"Don't play with fire, Chère, you'll only get burned."

He stood, then walked to the door.

"Jake," she called after him, then went nearer. "Don't go."

His shoulders tensed.

"I'm tired of being alone," she said. "Day after day, you leave me. Is my company so...difficult?"

"Don't you understand, Ana? I'm trying to do the right thing. You have a life somewhere else. When you leave here, I don't want you to have...regrets."

"I already have regrets, Jake.... I regret that I don't remember who I am. But I will never regret anything we share during our time together." Her breathing grew ragged. She was so angry she wanted to cry.

She marched out the door, without a clue as to where she was going.

And she didn't care.

Dear Reader,

There's no better escape than a fun, heartwarming love story from Silhouette Romance. So this August, be sure to treat yourself to all six books in our sexy, sizzling collection guaranteed to keep you glued to your beach chair.

Dive right into our fantasy-filled A TALE OF THE SEA adventure with Melissa McClone's *In Deep Waters* (SR#1608). In the second installment in the series about lost royal siblings from a magical kingdom, Kayla Waterton searches for a sunken ship, and discovers real treasure in the form of dark, seductive, modern-day pirate Captain Ben Mendoza.

Speaking of dark and seductive, Carol Grace's *Falling for the Sheik* (SR#1607) features the mesmerizing but demanding Sheik Rahman Harun, who is nursed back to health with TLC from his beautiful American nurse, Amanda Reston. Another royal has a heart-wrenching choice to make in *The Princess Has Amnesia!* (SR#1606) by award-winning author Patricia Thayer. She survived a jet crash in the mountains, but when the amnesia-stricken princess remembers her true social standing, will she—can she—forget her handsome rescuer…?

Myrna Mackenzie's *Bought by the Billionaire* (SR#1610) is a Pygmalian story starring Ethan Bennington, who has only three weeks to transform commoner Maggie Todd into a lady. While Cole Sullivan, the hunky, all-American hero in Wendy Warren's *The Oldest Virgin in Oakdale* (SR#1609), is coerced into teaching shy Eleanor Lippert how to seduce any man—himself included.

Then laugh a hundred laughs with Carolyn Greene's *First You Kiss 100 Men…* (SR#1611), a hilarious and highly sensual read about a journalist assigned to kiss 100 men. But there's only one man she *wants* to kiss….

Happy reading—and please keep in touch!

Mary-Theresa Hussey

Mary-Theresa Hussey
Senior Editor

Please address questions and book requests to:
Silhouette Reader Service
U.S.: 3010 Walden Ave., P.O. Box 1325, Buffalo, NY 14269
Canadian: P.O. Box 609, Fort Erie, Ont. L2A 5X3

The Princess
Has Amnesia!

PATRICIA THAYER

SILHOUETTE *Romance*®

Published by Silhouette Books

America's Publisher of Contemporary Romance

Special thanks and acknowledgment are given
to Patricia Thayer for her contribution to the
CROWN AND GLORY series.

To all the other ladies in the CROWN AND GLORY series:

Libby, Allison, Chris, Cara, Karen, Maureen, Elizabeth and Barbara.
It was a pleasure to work with such talent. Hope we can do it again.

And to the two new men in my life, Harrison John and Griffin Thomas.
Your grandma loves you.

SILHOUETTE BOOKS

RECYCLED PAPER

ISBN 0-373-19606-7

THE PRINCESS HAS AMNESIA!

Copyright © 2002 by Harlequin Books S.A.

Visit Silhouette at www.eHarlequin.com

Printed in U.S.A.

Books by Patricia Thayer

Silhouette Romance

Just Maggie #895
Race to the Altar #1009
The Cowboy's Courtship #1064
Wildcat Wedding #1086
Reilly's Bride #1146
*The Cowboy's Convenient
   Bride* #1261
*_Her Surprise Family_ #1394
*_The Man, the Ring, the
   Wedding_ #1412
†*Chance's Joy* #1518
†*A Child for Cade* #1524
†*Travis Comes Home* #1530
The Princess Has Amnesia! #1606

Silhouette Special Edition

Nothing Short of a Miracle #1116
Baby, Our Baby! #1225
*_The Secret Millionaire_ #1252
Whose Baby Is This? #1335

*With These Rings
†The Texas Brotherhood

PATRICIA THAYER

has been writing for the past sixteen years and has published fifteen books with Silhouette. Her books have been nominated for the National Readers' Choice Award, Virginia Romance Writers of America's Holt Medallion and a prestigious RITA® Award. In 1997 *Nothing Short of a Miracle* won the *Romantic Times* Reviewers' Choice Award for Best Special Edition.

Thanks to the understanding men in her life—her husband of thirty years, Steve, and her three sons and two grandsons—along with her daughter-in-law, Pat has been able to fulfill her dream of writing romance. Another dream is to own a cabin in Colorado, where she can spend her days writing and her evenings with her favorite hero, Steve. She loves to hear from readers. You can write to her at P.O. Box 6251, Anaheim, CA 92816.

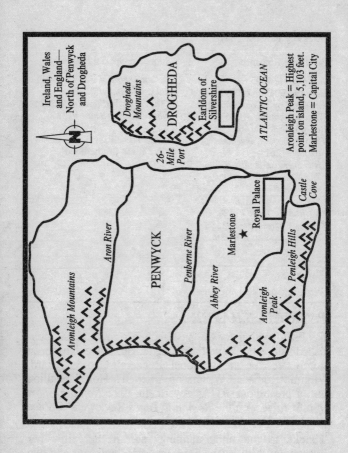

Ireland, Wales and England—North of Penwyck and Drogheda

N

Aronleigh Mountains

Aron River

PENWYCK

Penberne River

Abbey River

Aronleigh Peak

Marlestone

★

Royal Palace

Penleigh Hills

Castle Cove

26-Mile Port

Drogheda Mountains

DROGHEDA

Earldom of Silvershire

ATLANTIC OCEAN

Aronleigh Peak = Highest point on island, 5,103 feet. Marlestone = Capital City

Prologue

Fifty-mile-an-hour winds and driving rain had shut down the Penwyck Airport. All flights in or out had been cancelled because of the fierce storm. In the tower the air traffic controller tried desperately to contact the troubled jet that had taken off just before the closure. Perspiration beaded over his body as he frantically searched the screen for the signal.

Nothing.

"Royal Bird Two, repeat your location. Over." He spoke clearly into the microphone, then released the button praying for a miracle that the plane would reappear in his quadrant. Again he asked for verification. "Royal Bird Two repeat your location. Over." But outside of heavy static, there was only silence.

He swallowed back the dryness in his throat and repeated the request again, then again. There was no response from the royal family's jet.

He buzzed for help and his supervisor appeared immediately at his station. "Royal Bird Two has disappeared from our radar,'' he explained, trying to keep the trembling from his voice.

"What do you mean *disappeared?*" the supervisor asked, unable to hide his panic. "How can that be?"

"I'm not sure. The plane could have dropped in altitude…" They all knew the worst, but no one would speak of it. Tensions ran high in this type of job, but to lose the royal family's plane… "The last transmission from the jet was a request to change their flight pattern, hoping to get out of the weather. I cleared them, then suddenly they were gone."

The supervisor immediately picked up the phone and called the palace. After receiving his orders, he took the controller's seat and he tried to make contact himself. But he couldn't summon the missing jet either.

Not ten minutes later the tower door swung open and three men rushed in. Their black suits were meant to make them blend in with the crowd, but just by their stature and presence alone, they stood out. They wore badges that proclaimed them members of the Royal Elite Team. One of the men, Jack Harrison, approached the control module and everyone stepped back. His expression was deadly serious as he glared at the supervisor.

"We have a Priority One situation here. So we will go over everything, step by step," he ordered, then pointed out the window at the raging storm. "Princess Anastasia is out there somewhere and we have to find her."

Chapter One

The Lear jet vibrated from turbulence as Anastasia Penwyck's grip tightened on the armrest of her seat. Under normal circumstances, she didn't mind flying, but this roller-coaster ride was not to her liking. Not at all.

Maybe it had been foolish of her to go off to London in such weather, but with all the madness going on at the palace recently, Ana had put her own projects aside too long. The needs of the children who had come to depend on her were important. Now that Owen had been safely returned home, she couldn't delay what she had to do. Even if it meant she had to be up at the ungodly hour of 5:00 a.m.

It had taken some doing to convince her mother of the urgency of the trip. As a member of the royal family, Ana's safety was always a concern. Her father, King Morgan of Penwyck, had taught her to be aware and alert. These days he had a new battle of his own to fight. For his life. Even though he was receiving the best medical care, she hated leaving him when he was still in a coma. Ana also knew the king wouldn't want his daughter to neglect her duties.

The orphanage Marlestone House was one of Ana's latest campaigns, and she would do anything to help these abandoned children. One of her favorite things was teaching them to ride. She'd already moved several of the palace's gentlest horses to the home and had been giving instructions. Best of all, the media knew nothing of this. Dressed in jeans and a baseball cap, she was known to the children only as "Annie."

But a six-year-old named Catherine couldn't ride. Two years before, the girl's leg had been badly mangled in an accident and never healed correctly. Ana's search for someone to help led her to London's top orthopedic surgeon, Dr. Thor Havenfield. A busy man, he'd informed Ana that he could meet with her before rounds at the hospital.

The plane shook again and Ana drew in a breath. Why was she so nervous? The pilot was experienced and they weren't far from the mainland. She looked out the window, searching for the Welsh coastline, but visibility was nil. Maybe she should have waited for the weather to clear.

More turbulence! When it settled down for a moment Ana heard the pilot talking with the tower, then she felt the plane change course, but not soon enough. Lightning flashed, followed by a horrendous thunderclap. The jet shook violently this time.

Ana heard the orders being tossed back and forth between the men in the cockpit. Then there was a different tearing sound. Something was wrong with one of the engines. The jet tilted as they began to lose altitude.

Ana's heart beat wildly. Oh, God! What was happening?

Her bodyguard, Rory, peered at her from the cockpit. "We've lost an engine, but we're going to try and land the plane," he said. "Grab some cushions from the benches and stuff them around you. Then put your head in your lap."

"Rory, please," she pleaded. "Tell me the truth. Are we going to…make it?"

He smiled. "I won't let anything happen to you, Princess."

The jet vibrated in earnest, sounding like it was breaking apart. Anastasia closed her eyes and thought about her family…. All her regrets. All the things she put off in her life. Twenty-five years was too short a time. She would never know what it was like to truly fall in love. A tear found its way down her cheek as she heard the pilot shouting.

"Mayday! Mayday! This is Royal Bird Two. We've lost power and we're going to attempt to land."

Ana buried her head in the cushions, and held on tight and prayed. Then came the awful sounds, the screeching of metal, the breaking glass, a series of sudden hard bumps and jerks. The force threatened to throw her from her seat, but her seat belt stopped her. Then the sound of her own screams…then nothing….

He can only watch as she runs toward the car. There's nothing he can do to stop her. He tries to go after her, but something or someone is holding him back.

Terror races through him. She's walking into a trap. No! No! Meg! "Don't go," he yells, but his words are only a hoarse whisper. Then a sudden explosion rocks the ground, throwing him backward as orange flames and debris shoot out in all directions, the heat scorching his skin and hair.

With a gasp, Jake Sanderstone jerked up in his bed. Sweat beaded along his naked body as he fought to pull air into his constricted lungs. Nothing worked until he began the calming exercises the doctor had recommended. Soon his breathing slowed along with his heart rate.

That was when he realized the fierce rain pounding against the cabin's roof, and Max's frantic barking. Combing his fingers through his hair, he stood and walked into the main room. Although not quite dawn, he could see the five-year-old shepherd mix pawing the floor by the door.

Lightning flashed again and seconds later thunder crashed, rumbling through the wooden structure. "Okay, I'll let you out."

Jake unlocked the rough fir door and pulled it open, allowing the cold wind in, sending a chill through his body. But it felt good. Made him feel alive. Not that he deserved to be. A rush of sadness threatened to swamp him, instead he dragged himself back to reality as the dog scampered outside.

Hearing a noise that didn't sound related to the storm, Jake went to the edge of the porch and looked up in the sky. Off in the distance, he saw a light then made out the distinctive sound of a jet engine winding down. A pilot himself, he realized the plane was in trouble and coming down…fast. And there was nowhere to land in these mountains.

Damn! All he could do was watch as the small jet dropped out of sight, then heard a crash and the huge golden glow as flames shot up in the air. The impact and his previous training threw Jake into automatic rescue mode. He had to get out there and see if there were any survivors.

Jake rushed inside and pulled on special insulated clothing to protect him from the hard elements. There would be no rescue helicopter to help in this remote area. He was the only one. And since the area the plane went down was treacherous, he had to go in on foot. He grabbed his jacket and a backpack filled with a flashlight and other necessities for hiking, then hurried outside.

"Okay, Max." Jake pulled on his cap. "Lead the way."

As if the dog understood him, he took off through the brush. Jake kept up, all the time hoping that when they got to their destination, there would be a chance for survivors. The rain had slowed to a steady drizzle, but the thick foliage made the going rough through the forest. Still unfamiliar with the area after only four months, Jake trusted Max's instincts. It was just over the rise when he inhaled the faint odor of fuel and smoke. Then he saw the row of damaged trees that the jet clipped off as it came into the meadow. Fifty yards beyond was the wreckage. Pieces of the aircraft had scattered when it broke apart on impact.

Jake arrived at the cockpit first to see it had taken the brunt of the crash. The fire was out and there were two men still strapped in their seats. He reached through the shattered glass and checked each man's pulse. Nothing. Not that he'd expected any. He hurried on to the midsection that had separated and rested ten yards back. He checked inside, no one. Max sniffed around, then went outside, but Jake knew that someone had been sitting in one of the seats because there was fresh blood. Max began barking again.

Jake followed the sound until he caught up with the animal as he scurried through the trees. Again the rain grew heavy as Max began to bark in earnest. Jake found the dog in a group of trees. He was standing beside a body.

Jake knelt down beside Max. "Good, boy," he praised as he went to the survivor. He took in the soaked jacket and skirt and dainty bare feet. A woman. Gently, he rolled her over and brushed her wet hair from her face. He tried to ignore the pretty face he exposed, but even with the large bump on her head, she was striking. He checked for a pulse and found one, a little weak, but she was alive. He was examining for broken bones and any other injuries when she moaned, then opened her eyes to reveal a rich blue color.

Her lips trembled. "Fire... Please... Help me," she whispered.

"I'll do my best, ma'am," he said, taking the blanket from his pack and covering her cold body. He figured she'd been exposed for the past thirty minutes. They had a little protection from the rain where they were, but how bad was the storm going to get? The crashed plane wasn't any protection either, since it was in a ravine and the heavy rain could cause flooding. He needed to get her back to the cabin and take care of her. He could deal with the others later.

He tucked the blanket over her soaked skirt and jacket. She definitely wasn't dressed for a hike in the mountains, nor was she in any shape to. Her pupils were dilated, meaning she had a concussion. Besides, she'd been exposed to the cold rain too long. He needed to get her dry and warm. Now.

He brought her to a sitting position. "Come on, wake up."

She blinked and stared up at him.

"I need to get you out of the weather. So that means I'll have to carry you. It may hurt, but I'll try and be as gentle as possible."

No answer. Her eyes drifted shut once again.

He smiled as his hands moved to her small waist and he lifted her up and over his right shoulder in a fireman's carry. He heard her groan and regretted his roughness, but this was the only way he could get her back to the cabin.

By the time he reached the door, they were both soaked to the skin and his legs were cramping from exhaustion. He stumbled inside and went straight to the couch in front of the fireplace and gently laid her down. Then he began tossing wood onto the grate, and set a match to the kindling. Once the fire caught, he turned back to his charge. She looked pale, and when he touched her face her skin was ice-cold.

Jake stripped off the blanket, then went to work on the expensive little blue suit that hadn't provided much protection against the heavy rain. He unfastened the zipper, and slid the soaked material down her narrow hips, revealing long shapely legs. Next came the jacket and fancy silk blouse.

He drew in a breath when he got to the lacy underwear. Suddenly the room seemed warm. Lord! He'd been in the mountains too long if he sunk to ogling an unconscious woman. He went into the bedroom, stripped the dry blanket off the bed. Returning, he draped it over her.

With her covered, he took off the remainder of her wet clothes. After placing the articles of clothing by the fire, he took a few minutes to change into a pair of fresh jeans and a flannel shirt, which he left unbuttoned as he busied himself getting a pot of coffee started on the woodstove. He dried off Max and gave the dog some food, but decided to check the horses later.

Suddenly the woman cried out and he rushed back to the couch.

"No! No! Rory!"

"Hush," he coaxed. "It's okay." She finally settled down. Who was Rory? Her husband? He looked down at her ringless finger, which didn't mean she wasn't married or engaged.

He cleaned and bandaged her head wound, then poured some coffee into a mug and went back to her. He managed to get a few sips into her, but she wouldn't stop shivering.

After securing the blanket around her, he picked her up and carried her closer to the fire. He sat down with her on his lap. When he went to lay her on the rug, she moved closer against him.

"C-cold," she whispered through her trembling. "So cold."

"I know, I'm trying my best to remedy the situation." He reached out and brushed the damp hair from her face.

God, she was beautiful. Her oval-shaped face was only perfected by her features, her large blue eyes, straight nose and delicate jaw adorned with a slightly dimpled chin. His gaze lowered to her mouth. Full and pouty, her lips had a rosy hue that was not only inviting…but way too tempting.

He fought off the enticement and discovered a fine gold chain hanging around her slender neck. Attached to it was a charm of some kind. He picked up the amulet to discover the finely scripted letters, *A-N-A.*

"Is Ana your name or your initials?" He checked her pupils again. They were dilated. "Come on, Miss Ana, you need to wake up for me."

She groaned again, but only burrowed deeper into his chest. Somehow she worked the blanket from around her slim body and her bare skin pressed against the opening in his shirt. He sucked in a breath, trying not to think about the last time he had held a woman in his arms. But his body told him it had been far too long.

As much as he longed for some company besides Max, something told him that this beautiful woman was trouble for him. Suddenly the storm intensified. The sound of rain pounding on his roof let him know he was going to have a houseguest for a while. There was no way anyone was leaving this mountain any time soon.

She moved against him again. He closed his eyes and held back a groan as her breasts brushed against his chest. There was no breathing exercises in the world to help him now.

"Come on, sugar," he said as his southern breeding slipped out. "Have a heart. I'm only human. Wake up and save yourself. Save the both of us."

She could hear a man's voice. A deep voice that was calling to her, but she couldn't move, and her head hurt, so much that she felt tears in her eyes. Why did he want to hurt her?

She heard his voice again. "Ana, wake up."

Ana? Who was Ana? She tried to remember, but her mind couldn't recall anything. Another pain shot through her body as she tried to move. She cried out and felt a gentle touch accompany the man's soothing words, along with the warmth of his breath against her face.

She fought to make her eyes open, but she couldn't manage it. Frustration exhausted her when she couldn't perform that simple task. She wanted to scream but was too weak. More tears made their way down her cheeks. Again she felt them being brushed away.

"Ssh, don't cry. I'm here."

Who was here? Please, let me wake up, she pleaded as the man's voice faded in and out. Finally she managed to force her eyes open. Things were blurry, but she could make out the outline of a man's head topped with black hair. She blinked again and he started coming into focus.

The first thing she noticed about him was his nearly black eyes, deep set with tiny lines fanning out from the corners. More lines etched his forehead, showing his concern.

"So you decided to wake up." He smiled and her breath caught in her throat.

"What happened?" she asked as panic filled her. "Where am I?" She tried to look around, but the slightest movement caused her pain.

"Whoa, slow down. You had a rough time of it. You have a concussion."

Again she tried to move and that was when she realized she was naked and he was holding her against his body. Instantly, her breasts tingled with the contact and her nipples hardened. The startled look on his face told her that he was aware of the situation, too.

Fighting the pain, she pushed against his chest. "Get away from me," she ordered. "How dare you?" She grabbed at the blanket and covered herself as best she could, not wanting to lose any more dignity. "I demand to know why you took off my clothes."

The man stiffened, then slowly relaxed. He raised his jean covered leg and draped his arm across his knee and nodded to the fire where her wet clothes were spread out on the bricks drying.

"By the time I got you back to the cabin, you were soaked from the rain," he said. "The only way to keep you from getting hypothermia was to remove your wet clothes and bring your body temperature up to normal. You'd been exposed to the elements for over an hour."

She was confused. What was she doing out in this weather? She looked around the small room. It was roughly furnished with a sofa and rocking chair, and a multicolored braided rug covered the plank floor. She had no idea where she was.

She turned back to the stranger. "Who are you?"

"My name is Jake Sanderstone." He offered his hand. "And you are…?"

She blinked and thought, but try as she might she couldn't come up with a name…nothing. "I don't know."

Chapter Two

"I don't know who I am," she said, still not believing it.

She closed her eyes and willed herself to remember something. Blank. Nothing. It was as if someone had erased everything in her brain. And she had absolutely no idea who she was. She looked at the stranger. "How can that be?"

His dark eyes studied her. "I'd say that nasty bump on your head might have something to do with it. You've been through a lot in just a few hours."

She reached up and touched the tender area. "How did I get it?" One of a thousand questions she needed answers to. "How did I get *here?* Oh, God! Where am I?"

"Now, slow down. I'll tell you as much as I can," he promised. "You're in a remote part of the Cambrian Mountains in Wales. Your plane lost power and came in for a crash landing." He nodded toward the German shepherd lying by the fire. "Max woke me up and we tracked the location. By the time we got to the crash sight, you had wandered off. It took us awhile to find you, but thanks to Max again, we located you under some trees. Then I brought you back here to the cabin.''

Then he stripped her naked, she thought. None of what the man said stirred her memory. ''Surely there was someone with me. Please, don't tell me I was flying the plane.''

He glanced away, then back to her. ''No, there were two men inside, the pilot and copilot. I'm sorry. They didn't make it. As far as I know, you're the only survivor.''

Dead. Two people were dead. She waited to feel something for the men, but nothing. She was almost ashamed of her lack of emotions. The victims could have been her friends, or members of her family.

Jake got to his feet and walked to the stove. He wanted to give her some space to sort things out. She'd had a terrible shock. Not only had her plane fallen out of the sky, she might have lost someone special to her. And when her memory returned, she'd have a lot to deal with. Something he knew about all too well.

''Did I have a wallet on me, or something that had any identification?'' She looked like a waif as she brushed her tangled brown hair from her face and clutched the warm blanket like a lifeline. She was so damn appealing he had trouble speaking.

''I didn't have much time to search the plane. The storm had worsened and once I found you, I thought best to get you somewhere dry. The temperature dropped ten degrees before we made it back here. You were pretty chilled. The only thing you have that might give a clue to your name is the charm around you neck. There are three initials, A.N.A., or it could also stand for the name Ana.''

She frowned. ''Can we call the police or a forest ranger? Somebody?''

''Not possible. You picked a remote place to land. I have an off-road vehicle, but the road here washed out yesterday when this storm hit.''

''How will anyone find me?'' Panic clouded her eyes, along with pain.

''If your pilot radioed his location, someone should be looking for you. But that could take a few days with these conditions.''

Jake turned to the sink, grabbed the pump handle and primed it until water shot out of the faucet. This place didn't have any modern conveniences. Hell, it didn't even have many of the basics. That was the charm for Jake. To be as far away from the world and its problems as he could get. But it looked like one of them had found him.

He filled the glass, took two ibuprofen from the first-aid kit and walked back to her. ''Here, take these. They should help take the edge off.'' He offered her two tablets.

She looked confused.

''They're just over-the-counter painkillers. Can't hurt you. Go on, take them. Your head has to be killing you.''

''It's like someone's using it as a drum,'' she admitted, then took the medication and drank thirstily from the glass. She gave it back to him. ''Thank you. Now, if you wouldn't mind, I'd like to get dressed,'' she said haughtily. ''Would you please find me something to wear?'' She looked down at the blanket.

The burning wood in the fireplace crackled and sparks shot out. The last thing Jake needed was to be reminded she was naked underneath, especially since he was the one who helped her get in that condition. His fingertips still could recall the feel of her soft skin. *Forget it, Sanderstone, this woman's trouble. You don't mix well with the pampered princess type.*

"I hate to disappoint you, but until your clothes dry out all I can offer you is one of my shirts and a pair of sweatpants."

There was that defiant look again, then her features softened. "I'll be appreciative of anything you can lend me."

Jake went into the bedroom and pulled a faded chambray shirt from the closet and a pair of black sweatpants. He returned and handed the items to her.

She glanced around. "Is there some place I can wash up?"

"Sure. In the sink. But I wouldn't suggest you exert yourself just yet. Remember you have a concussion."

"I know I will feel much better if I can clean up some." She tried to stand, but stumbled.

Jake reached out and caught her as she was about to go down. He wrapped his arms around her, trapping the downward slide of the blanket. The cloth barely covered her breasts and their fullness threatened to spill out. *Oh, Lord help me.*

"Okay, let's get something straight. Until you can stand on your own, I'll take care of you."

"But…"

"There are no buts. I'm the boss here. If you want, I'll let you arm wrestle me for the job." He cocked an eyebrow to see how far she'd fight him.

"Not fair," she mumbled.

"Well, hell, who told you life is fair?" He knew firsthand how ugly it could be out there in the trenches, starting with a childhood that had been spent on the rough side of New Orleans.

He liked it better here…alone.

"If only I could remember…something, my name," she said.

"How about I just call you, sugar?" He grinned.

"Don't you dare. It sounds like a country-and-western song."

"Well, now is your chance. You pick a name."

She fingered the charm around her neck. "How about Ana?"

She looked up at him with those rich blue eyes and instantly he knew that was her name. It fit her. Fit her beauty…her courage…even her irritating stubbornness.

Never wavering from her mesmerizing gaze, he took the shirt and held it out for her. She managed to slip one arm into the sleeve while continuing to grasp the blanket. Then he wrapped the shirt around her back and she put her other arm in. He closed the front and did up the buttons. Once he finished, the blanket fell to the floor. Oh man, this woman was going to make him crazy. "I have socks for your feet."

He guided her to the couch and sat her down, then went back to the bedroom. He rummaged through his drawers and found the last clean pair of white athletic socks. He needed to do laundry. He returned to the couch to find his guest curled up on her side, sound asleep. She had gone through a lot of trauma this morning. Maybe it was a blessing she couldn't remember what happened in the crash. Life's tragedies often turned into nightmares.

Trying not to disturb her sleep, he worked the socks over her dirty, but delicate feet. There was dried mud on her calves too, but she could wash up later, he thought, tugging the white fabric up her shapely leg.

"Seems we're getting pretty familiar, sugar." He smiled, but didn't feel any mirth. She hadn't liked him calling her that. Good. It made her angry. That's exactly what he wanted. For her to stay distant and as far away from him as possible. He listened to the rain, hoping it would let up and things could get back to normal. That someone would come looking for the plane and her, soon.

It had been awhile since he had taken care of anyone. Not since his mother. Memories of their crummy apartment flooded his head. The smell of alcohol, his mother's slurred words as she tried to apologize for not bringing home any food for him. At only ten years old, he'd learned quickly to fend for himself, not to depend on anyone.

Jake had made a point of being independent. Meg had been the closest he'd come to a relationship and that had been a mistake, too. They'd been partners in the bureau. He was a twelve-year veteran. He should have seen the danger, he should have been able to save her. Instead, he let his guard down and allowed her to walk into a trap.

Pain and regret washed over him, constricting his chest as he watched the mystery woman sleep. He didn't want to be responsible for anyone again. That's why he'd come here. Far away from country and duty, to figure out his plans for the rest of his life. All he knew was that his career with the bureau was over. He'd specialized in terrorism and worked undercover. He had seen too much ugliness and total disregard for human life. He just hadn't had the stomach for it anymore. After handing in his resignation, he'd had no trouble walking away.

Through an acquaintance, he'd heard about Wales. So he packed up and traveled to the Welsh countryside. He liked hiking in the mountains. Then he'd found this remote cabin where he could be by himself, and over the past four months, he'd been able to get through most days. He still had the nightmares and he'd gotten lonely some times, but he was staying.

He covered his guest with a blanket and put another log on the fire, then walked out the door to feed the horses. He only hoped that he was going to get back his solitude. Real soon.

"Wake up, Ana. Come on. Open those pretty blues for me."

Ana stirred and tried to shove at the hand on her arm. "Go away."

"Sorry, can't do that."

Her head was pounding as she rolled over. "Go away, Rory. I want to sleep."

"Can't do that," he said, in a voice that was low and smooth as velvet. "So Rory will have to wait."

Slowly Ana came out of her fog and she opened her eyes. The man before her was familiar, but he represented what she didn't want to remember. A plane crash, two dead men and no memory of who she was or if anyone was even looking for her.

"What do you want?"

"I need to check your pupils," he said.

She slowly and carefully made it into a sitting position, mainly to get away from him. "What?"

"Your eyes. You have a concussion. I let you sleep a few hours, but you need to be awake now."

"Okay, I'm awake." She looked toward the door. "Is it still raining?" Silly question when she could see water sheeting off the window pane.

"It eased off for a while."

She looked back at the man. "How do you stand being up here by yourself?"

He shrugged. "I like being alone."

"Yes, solitude can have its advantages, but what if something happened?"

"Max is a pretty good watchdog, he could go for help."

That sparked an idea in her head. "Could he go now and let the authorities know I'm here?"

"Not in this weather. Besides, this isn't a life-or-death situation."

"Maybe not to you," she said, hating the trapped feeling that was enveloping her.

"If you'll be patient a while, this weather will clear and I'll get you down the mountain, or better yet, maybe *Rory* will rescue you."

"*Rory?* Who's Rory?"

"You tell me. You called out his name when I tried to wake you."

She gasped. "I did?" At his nod, she worked to remember, but nothing came. She couldn't come up with anyone by the name of Rory. What if he was her...husband? "I can't remember," she said through gritted teeth.

"Stop trying so hard. Things will come to you." He moved closer. "Now, look up here so I can check your pupils.'' She did as he asked and sat still as he shined the flashlight in her eyes.

Jake Sanderstone was so close that she could feel his breath against her face. She drew air into her lungs and inhaled his scent and something else. Straw and some kind of animal. A horse.

She pulled back. ''Horses.''

''What?'' He looked confused and annoyed. ''What about horses?''

''You smell like horses. Why is that?''

His nearly black eyes captured hers. ''Maybe because I just came in from feeding two in the stable. Why? Do you remember something?''

She shook her head. ''Just that I recognize the scent of horses. That's not such a breakthrough. Pretty distinctive odor.''

''Maybe. But you might know something about horses. Give yourself some time to think about that.'' He got up and went to the kitchen area. On the stove was a pan and he began stirring. ''If you're hungry, I heated up some stew.''

Suddenly, her stomach growled. ''Maybe I could eat a little.''

''Good.'' He smiled this time. ''It'll help you get your strength back.'' He pulled down two mismatched bowls from the cupboard and filled them with two large ladle full of stew. He carried the heaping bowls to the small table and went back for a loaf of bread.

''Supper is ready,'' he said as he came to the couch.

Ana started to stand, but her legs wouldn't cooperate. Instead of asking for his help, she used the couch for support and slowly made her way into the kitchen. "Looks good."

"It's canned. I'm hoping when you feel better, you can practice your culinary skills on me."

"I don't cook."

He sent her a questioning look. "Now, of all the things you had to remember, why that?"

She shrugged and picked up her spoon. "I don't think I've spent much time in a kitchen at all." She paused and looked around the bowl.

"What are you looking for?"

"A napkin."

Silently, Jake went to the cupboard and pulled out a package of paper napkins and handed her one. She could feel his eyes on her as she placed it across her lap.

"You all set now?" he asked as he returned to his seat.

"Yes, thank you," she answered. After taking a bite, she savored the taste. She'd probably had better, but nothing more appreciated. "As I was saying…I don't recognize anything."

"Well, when you're feeling better, I'll introduce you around," he said with a cocky smile, then added, "sugar."

"I insist you stop calling me by that ridiculous name."

"You're insisting?"

Ana hated that flash of arrogance in his midnight eyes. She didn't like being teased, never did. Another flicker of memory. Well, she wasn't about to tell him that so she concentrated on eating her stew. But there was another pressing matter that she did have to talk with him about. She needed to use the facilities. She looked around the room wondering if it was through the bedroom.

"What do you need?" he asked her.

"Nothing." She turned back to her food, but the need wouldn't go away, it only intensified. She stood. "Would you please direct me to the facilities?"

"Sure, but I'm going to have to go with you."

"I beg your pardon. I assure you Mr. Sanderstone, I'm capable of taking care of the situation quite nicely, thank you."

"The name's Jake. And I think this time, especially in your condition, you need my help."

"You've helped quite enough. Now I want you to show me where to go."

His smile turned into a full-fledged grin. "It would be my pleasure." He pointed to the door. "It's outside to the left about thirty yards from the cabin."

Ana bit back a groan, but wouldn't give him the satisfaction of seeing her distaste. He went to the door ahead of her and helped her into rain gear and boots. He opened the door and walked her to the edge of the porch. He turned serious. "Sure you don't need my help, sugar?"

Her temper flared again. "Look…*Yank.* I told you, I can handle this."

She got the satisfaction of seeing his irritation before she stepped off the porch. The cold rain washed over her face and made her shiver. She moved slowly, but she would die before she let Jake Sanderstone know just how much she really needed him.

Just before dawn the next morning, Jake was stretched out on the couch, listening to the crackling of the fire. Ana had gone to sleep in the bed. He'd checked on her off and on during the night. She was much better. Enough so he felt he could leave her for a while.

After hours of deliberating, he'd come to the conclusion that he had to return to the crash site. There were two bodies up there exposed to animals and the elements, and he needed to bury them.

There also might be a chance that the plane's radio still worked. A slim one, but it would be great if he could at least get word out about the crash and the lone survivor. Not that there was any chance that a rescue team would get here until the storm passed and that could be days away. But he had to try.

And it wouldn't hurt to find out about the woman he'd brought into his home. Maybe he could find some information on her in the meantime. At least she would have a name and maybe that would help trigger her memory.

He threw back his blanket and stood. He grabbed his dried pants from the hearth and put them on, next came his shirt and a sweater. He went to the sink and pumped water and splashed some on his face. The cold made him shiver. Well, if that didn't wake him nothing would. Not wanting to waste any time, he'd eat breakfast on the trail and reached in the cupboard for some jerky.

He grabbed his jacket then rubbed Max's fur "Come on, boy, I have a job for you," he whispered and led him into the bedroom.

He stood next to the bed. Ana was asleep on her side, her hair nearly covering her face. He brushed the strands away and she moaned and rolled over on her back. She blinked at him, then opened her eyes.

"You again," she groaned. "Don't you ever get

tired of disturbing my sleep? Fine, do what you have to do."

Jake closed his eyes a moment and tried to erase the dangerous thoughts in his head. "I wanted you to know that I'll be gone for a few hours. Max will be here for you. So you'll be safe. There's plenty of wood for the fire. It's best if you stay in bed." And out of trouble, he finished to himself.

All he got from her was the soft sound of her even breathing. She was great for the male ego, he thought ironically. Well, when he got back he would know who she was, and with any luck, she'd be gone soon. He put on his rain gear, walked out the door, locked it, then grabbed the shovel from the side of the cabin and headed toward the ridge. In a few days he'd be all alone again.

And that's just the way he liked it.

Chapter Three

The trip took him nearly thirty minutes, but Jake made the climb over the ridge without much problem. The rain had finally slowed, and he hoped it would stay that way until he finished his task.

When he reached the edge of the ravine, he paused, amazed at the destruction. Entire rows of trees had been bent or broken off by the force of the jet, but in the end, the mountain won out.

His gaze lowered to the yards and yards of debris scattered along the ground. He walked past what was left of the tail, then to the plane's fuselage, and the twisted metal was all that was left of the wings. They'd been stripped away as if the plane were a toy. Only the midsection remained intact and that was where Ana had been seated. Jake glanced inside and saw the cushions that she'd placed around her; the padding must have saved her in the crash.

He quickly moved on. A job needed to be done before he could look for any clues about his guest. It could be days before anyone arrived to investigate the accident. Jake had to be careful not to disturb too much, but he couldn't just leave the bodies unprotected, either. He walked about twenty yards up the slope to a pine tree, removed his backpack and picked up the shovel.

About an hour later, he'd finished his digging. Ignoring his fatigue, he returned to the plane and removed the first body from the cockpit. He took the man's ID from his pocket. In bold black letters it proclaimed him to be, Rory Hearne, Penwyck security, top priority clearance.

"Rory," he said the name aloud. "So you're the one she called out for in the night." Jake experienced a tightening in his gut that felt suspiciously like jealousy. That was crazy. He didn't even know the woman. Why would he care if she and this Rory were lovers?

Jake lifted the other man from his seat and retrieved his ID. He found a pilot's license for Stephen Loden also from Penwyck. That wouldn't be out of the ordinary since the small island of Penwyck wasn't too far off the coast of Wales.

After tucking Rory's gun into his belt and the wallets into his jacket pocket, he started to lift the pilot and noticed a small tattoo through the tear in his shirt. A small, black sword. Where had he seen that tattoo before? During his years with the bureau, Jake had accumulated a lot of miscellaneous information, read over hundreds of advisory reports. As a terrorism specialist, his life had depended on it.

A sword. Jake searched his memory. The black sword represented the Black Knights. That was it. The

Black Knights were a subversive group located in Europe.

Now he wanted to know what a security guard with top clearance and a pretty blue-eyed girl, with no memory were doing with a rebel. He had a lot of questions to ask his guest when he got back to the cabin.

She woke up with a killer headache, desperate to find something to stop the pounding. Climbing out of bed, she found the dog at her feet.

"Hello, fellow. Where's your master?" Not that she wanted to deal with the rude man, but she needed medication.

Still in the blue shirt that he'd given her, she gingerly walked to the door of the bedroom and opened it. There was a small fire in the hearth, but the room was deserted. Grimacing, she made her way to the kitchen area and located the first-aid kit.

Trembling with relief, she popped open the lid and found the bottle of aspirin. She removed two tablets, then took a glass from the cupboard. Pumping the water was a little difficult, but she managed. After swallowing the tablets, she went into the sitting area by the dying fire. My word, she was cold. There was a blanket on the back of the couch. She wrapped it around her shoulders and a familiar male scent suddenly filled her nostrils. She could smell him. Sitting down on the cushion, she burrowed into the warmth and closed her eyes.

She could picture the brooding man, dressed in a plaid shirt and jeans, his face drawn, tiny brackets lining the corners of his mouth. His straight white teeth were visible when he smiled, which was a rare occurrence. It was his beautiful raven-colored eyes that drew her attention, but the sadness she saw nearly broke her heart. What had happened in his life that made him want to live off by himself? A woman? What kind of woman was the man attracted to? Blondes…brunettes?

She reached for a strand of hair. Hers was light brown. Plain light brown. Did someone think she was attractive? Was someone out there missing her, aching for her to come home? She tried so hard to remember, but there were only blank spaces. Was there no one for her? She had been in limbo for the past two days. What was worse, her rescuer, Mr. Sanderstone, didn't want her around. Well, she didn't care. The Yank was bloody annoying. He was also handsome and very well built. What a pity he didn't have any manners, any polish.

A splattering of heavy raindrops hit the window, and she stared out the cloudy pane at the storm. Would she ever be able to leave here?

Suddenly there was pounding on the door. She got up and walked over, hesitating on her next move. Then she heard a familiar voice. "Hey, open up, it's raining like hell out here."

She unlatched the bolt and swung open the door to find Jake. He was soaked to the skin and he looked angry.

"Where have you been?" she asked.

He pushed passed her, stripped off his rain gear and hung it up on the hook "I've been up on the ridge, burying your friends."

She gasped. "My friends? Do you know who I am?"

"Sorry, I didn't have time to look around to learn

your name. The weather turned on me. After I buried the bodies, I had to start back.'' He took a chair from the table, sat down and started pulling off his wet boots. He jerked off his sweater, then unbuttoned his shirt as he tugged it from his pants.

With his black hair plastered against his head, he reached for a towel in the kitchen and mopped the water from his face and hair as he walked to the hearth. He looked at the fire and cursed. ''Couldn't you at least keep the fire going while I was gone?'' He removed the screen and placed several logs on the dying embers.

''I wasn't informed that you had left. And there were no written instructions telling me to keep anything going.''

''Common sense would tell you to add logs to the fire when it's going out.''

''You seem to forget that I was in a plane crash yesterday and I don't have any memory,'' she snapped. When she stood, her head began to spin and she swayed.

Alarmed, Jake rushed to her side. ''Whoa.'' He grabbed her by the arm, led her to the couch and sat her down. Damn. What was wrong with him? He was being a jerk.

''Does your head hurt?'' Stupid question. He could see the pain in her eyes.

''Yes, I took some medication from the first-aid kit.''

''Then rest here.''

''No,'' she said, refusing to lie back. ''I want to know what you found at the plane. Who...died?''

He shook his head. ''We can talk about it later when you're feeling better.''

"I need to know now," she demanded. "Who were they?"

He didn't want to go over this now, but it looked like he didn't have a choice. "There was a Rory Hearne, he was a security guard from Penwyck. Do you remember him?"

She shook her head again. "No."

"You sure? You cried out his name last night when I tried to wake you. It seems you were pretty familiar with this guy."

She frowned. "What are you insinuating, Mr. Sanderstone?"

He didn't like the feeling that had creeped back into his gut. "I'm only stating facts, chère."

"Well, stop it. You act as if I'm guilty of something. What if this Rory and I were…together? Is there any reason we shouldn't have been?"

"No, but we're trying to find out who you are." He was pushing her, but since his discovery, this situation had grown a lot more serious. And he needed some answers. "Does the name Stephen Loden ring any bells?"

She shook her head. "Was he the other man in the plane?"

Jake nodded.

"I want to thank you for burying them. That was kind of you."

"Forget it. I did what needed to be done."

"It was more than anyone could have expected of you, especially in this weather."

He got up. "Okay, I'm a nice guy." He started toward the bedroom. "I'm going to change my clothes."

Once inside the room, he shut the door harder than

needed, but his frustration drove him to it. He jerked off the wet shirt along with his undershirt. He was soaked to the skin. Peeling off his wet jeans was more difficult, but he managed. Opening the dresser drawer, he took out underwear and another pair of jeans.

What was he going to do now? He'd come here to Wales to get away from complications like this. And he'd had one big problem dropped in his lap. But this one was attached to a gorgeous woman with an attitude.

Not to mention a pair of legs that made his mouth water.

By the third day, Jake had cabin fever.

For the first time since he'd arrived in the mountains four months ago he wanted to leave. Thanks to one blue-eyed intruder, his peace and quiet—not to mention his solitude—was a thing of the past.

Why should it matter so much if he had a visitor for a few days? The cabin sure as hell wasn't big, but two rooms should be enough for two people. He wasn't so much of a bastard he couldn't share his space…for a while. Unless, of course, the other person was a woman who seemed set on driving him crazy.

''Yank indeed,'' he muttered, watching the continuing downpour through the window. Seventy-two hours had passed since he found his visitor, and as soon as this damn storm was over, he would take her down to the authorities and hand her off. But not before he satisfied his own curiosity and found out who his cabin mate was. Especially not until he found out what she was doing with a member of a known terrorist group.

He glanced across the room to Ana. Awake for the past thirty minutes, she sat quietly at the hearth, studying the fire and looking innocent. The shirt he'd given her to wear nearly swallowed her up. He could barely see her fingertips under the cuffs, which made her look fragile. He pushed aside any feelings of compassion as his gaze wandered down past the shirttails to her long, smooth legs. Another basic need surfaced and a surge of heat rushed through his body.

He growled a curse. She must have heard him because she looked up. Her hair, wild with curl, circled a pretty face, only marred by the bandage on her forehead. When their eyes locked and hers darkened like twin sapphires, he found his throat suddenly dry. Damn, she was gorgeous. Realizing that he was staring, he forced himself to look away, but his hunger stayed.

He couldn't let this woman get to him. Hell, she had a life somewhere. She could be involved in God knows what. So even if he wanted to pursue his interest, he couldn't let anything happen between them.

Her health had to be his main concern. "How is your head?"

"It still hurts."

"No doubt. You must have walloped yourself but good when the plane came down. You're lucky to have survived."

"Tell that to the two men who died."

"You're not responsible for their deaths."

Frowning, she stood. "Then why do I feel responsible? Why do I feel that they were taking *me* somewhere? You said I was the passenger and they were flying the plane."

"Yes, and one was a licensed pilot. Besides, the

plane had been cleared by the airport to take off.'' He came across the room and took a closer look into her rich enticing eyes, telling himself that he was only checking her pupils. They were normal. They had been for the past twenty-four hours. ''You can't keep second-guessing everything. It won't change a damn thing.''

''Well, it gives me something to think about since I don't have any other memories before yesterday. What do you do when you're by yourself around here? Besides go mad.''

He shrugged. ''There's plenty to do.''

She placed her hands on her hips. ''For instance?''

''Like fishing, or riding or hiking. This area is beautiful.''

''All I've seen is this room.'' Her eyes widened. ''And of course, the wonderful facilities out back.''

Jake was getting fed up with the woman's complaining. ''Well, you better head to those facilities once more, because it's about bedtime.''

''It's barely dark,'' she said.

''And we've both been up since long before daylight,'' he insisted.

''But I've slept all day. I'm not tired.''

''Well, I am.''

''Then you take the bed and I'll sleep out here.''

Damn, she was stubborn and he needed to get as far away from her as possible. He needed to be alone, even if he had to lock her in the bedroom to do it. He swung her up into his arms.

''Put me down this instant,'' she ordered.

Jake ignored her demand and carried her into the small room crowded with a double bed and dresser. He pulled back the blankets, then laid her down on top of the sheet. When she started to argue, he leaned over her and placed his finger against her lips. "Whether you know it or not, chère, you need to rest. You've been through a lot in the past two days."

All the fight seemed to leave her and she nodded. When she reached for his hand, her soft warmth made his gut tighten in a familiar and long denied need. A need he had pushed aside long ago.

"I can't keep taking your bed," she said. "What about you?"

Jake's desire flashed hotter and moved dangerously lower. Hell, he knew where he wanted to sleep, but he fought the crazy urge to climb in with her. "You're not taking anything, I'm offering." He moved back before he did something very foolish. "Besides, I want some time to myself. This way we won't disturb each other. I'll be fine on the couch." He sounded a little too gruff, but hell, she wouldn't leave it alone. "If you need anything holler."

"I'll have you know, Mr. Sanderstone, I've never 'hollered' in my life," she said indignantly, crossing her arms over her chest.

Jake wanted to laugh at his haughty houseguest. She looked distant and untouchable, but he knew that was far from the truth. He turned and left the room, hoping for a peaceful night. But he knew that peace wasn't possible as long as Ana was in the cabin.

Ana woke up the next morning and realized two things; she still couldn't remember who she was, and it was still raining. Climbing to her knees on the bed, she leaned against the adjacent windowpane and looked out at the heavily wooded forest. She'd had high hopes that today she would be able go outside.

And if the skies cleared, that would allow a rescue team to start searching for her.

But who would be searching? She had no idea. She closed her eyes and tried to force herself to remember, but there was nothing. Dear Lord, she had no idea how old she was. She tugged on the gold charm around her neck. Who had given it to her? A husband? She studied her bare ring finger. Who was Rory? Was he important to her?

Ana sat down on the bed and pulled her knees to her chest. What if she never regained her memory? Worse, what if no one was looking for her? In her head, she conjured up all kinds of scenarios, none of which helped calm her anxiety.

A loud knock broke through her reverie. Then the door swung open and Jake appeared. He had changed into a fresh pair of jeans and a blue and green flannel shirt. He'd washed up, too. His long hair was damp and his face free of any beard stubble.

He frowned. "You all right?"

She nodded and quickly blinked away her threatening tears.

"Don't give me that." Looking concerned, he walked to the bed and sat down next to her. "Are you in pain? Is it your head?"

"No, I'm feeling fine." She tried to turn away, but he wouldn't let her.

"You're not fine if you're crying."

"I'm not crying." She just felt like it. "I have a reason to be upset...I still can't remember anything." Now the tears rushed out along with the words.

"You need time. It'll happen," he promised. "It's only been a few days."

"It's been four." Ana suddenly felt weepy. She

hated weepy women. She'd never resorted to tears before, but now she couldn't seem to stop them.

Jake scooted closer on the bed and she breathed in the familiar scent of soap and the man. When his hands gripped her by the shoulders, she looked up at him. His coal-black eyes locked with hers, and she could see compassion and concern. A strange stirring erupted in her stomach, and she was oddly disappointed when he released her.

"Come on, chère, don't go all mushy on me."

She stiffened. "Mushy? I've got news for you, Yank. You'd be a little upset if you didn't even know your name."

His eyes turned dark and dangerous. "And I got news for ya'll. I'm not a *Yank* and never have been. I was born and raised in the south," he said with a heavy southern drawl. "Ya'll got that?"

She nodded, knowing better than to push him any farther.

"Good."

"And you may stop calling me silly pet names."

"Fine. Then you tell me what to call you."
She took hold of her charm. There wasn't much of a choice. "Call me Ana."

He stared at her. "Okay, Ana it is. Now, let's get some breakfast."

"Is that all you think about, food?"

He cocked his eyebrow and she caught a slight twitch at the corner of his mouth. She felt that strange feeling again.

"Believe me, I think about other things," he said in a husky voice. "But my stomach has been talking to me since before sunrise."

He tugged at her arm. "Come on, it's your turn to cook."

She resisted. "And I explained to you before that I don't know how. Besides, you seem very capable of doing the job."

"Well, capable or not, I'm tired of doing it. Your turn." He got her off the bed and into the other room. "If you need to make a trip to the *facilities,* you better be quick. I'm hungry."

Ana grumbled the whole time she put on her rainwear. She purposely took her time, but that didn't seem to change Jake's mood. When she returned to the cabin, he was leaning against the counter, waiting for her.

"You could have started without me. I'm not very hungry."

"Too bad, you need to eat and so do I. So don't think you're getting out of cooking. Since you seem to be recovered, we're going to share the chores."

"Maybe I should rest one more day, because of my head." She touched the bandage.

He paused, looking concerned. "You said it didn't hurt. Look, if you aren't feeling well, then go back to bed."

Here was her chance to get out of cooking, but something inside wouldn't let her lie. Besides, she'd be bored if she had to spend the day in bed.

"No, my health is fine," she said.

"Good." He led her over to the woodstove. Using a metal poker, he removed the round plate and exposed the fire below. After adding some more kindling, he replaced the cover.

"This baby is a little tricky, but when she gets going the place heats up fast."

Ana followed Jake's instructions. The food was simple. He had cooked her eggs in the past along with some ham.

"I have something special I brought along with me from the States." He held up a large box of pancake mix.

"Isn't that dessert?"

"Not where I come from," he said.

He showed her how to stir it all together. That was simple, the hard part came later. The first four pancake attempts she put on the griddle burned. Even Max turned his nose up at her efforts.

"I told you I can't do this," she complained.

She wanted to give up, but a persistent Jake wouldn't let her. "Come on, give it another try," he encouraged.

Again she poured more batter onto the griddle. Then, with Jake's hand over hers, guiding the spatula, they scooped up the cake and managed to flip it over and have it land back on the griddle.

"That's it," he cheered.

"They aren't burnt," she cried happily.

"A perfect golden brown," he said, then handed her a plate and she slid one cake after another off the griddle.

They sat down at the table with butter and syrup. After Ana watched Jake doctor his cakes, she did the same. She took a big bite.

"Oh, my, these are delicious." She swallowed and forked up another bite.

"You sure seem to be enjoying your breakfast. For someone who wasn't hungry, that is." He took a big bite of his own.

"I didn't know I was so hungry, or that these would taste so good."

"You've never had flapjacks before?"

She thought a moment, then shook her head. "I don't think so. Not like these." She took another bite and sighed in pleasure. "I remember something like this for dessert, a crepe."

"In the States we call these pancakes or flapjacks. In fact, we have restaurants that specialize in them. You can add several different ingredients—blueberries, bananas, strawberries, even chocolate chips."

She swallowed. "Chocolate. I love chocolate."

Jake paused to watch Ana. She was so animated. The stubborn, demanding woman was gone, for the time being anyway. He didn't want to think about all the other questions he wanted answers to. He wished he had never found out about the pilot's connection to the Black Knights, but he had, and that had only caused more complications. The most important; what was this woman's involvement?

Why should he even care? He was no longer a government agent, just a private citizen. When the rain stopped, he could take Ana to the authorities and let them handle things. Now he just had to deal with his attractive guest.

His staring caused her to pause. "What?"

"You...remembered you liked chocolate."

She looked thoughtful, then smiled. "I did, didn't I?"

"And more will come." He wondered if he should push. "Can you remember anything about being on the plane. Even the crash."

She shook her head. "No, I only remember hearing your voice, then waking up here."

He took the IDs from his pocket and handed them to her. "Look at these pictures, maybe something will come back."

She studied them for a long time. He couldn't see anything in her face that would help. Only a veil of sadness.

"I'm sorry." She gave them back to him. "I can't help you."

"It's hard to believe three strangers were passengers in that plane," he murmured more to himself.

She looked at him. "Why won't you believe me?"

He wanted to, but in his world, he'd learned the hard way not to trust. "It's not that I don't believe you don't have any memory of the crash. I'm a little confused about why you can't remember anything at all."

"So am I," she said. "And when I find the answer I'll let you know."

So the lady had sass. "I'd appreciate that."

"Thank you."

"For what?"

"For numerous things. For saving me. For feeding me." She took another bite, leaving a glaze of the syrup along her lips. Then just as quickly, she raised her napkin and gently dabbed at her mouth.

He glanced away, trying not to think about how much he wanted to lick away the sweet syrup. He blew out a breath to clear his head. "Next step is washing the dishes."

"No, I'm not finished. I want some more…flap-jacks."

Jake couldn't help but smile. "You want to go solo this time?"

She returned his smile. "I think I can manage it."

He was getting to like this side of Ana. A warning signal went up. Letting down his guard was not a good idea. He watched as she went to the stove, unable to remove his attention from her bare legs. The shirt he'd given her yesterday was big enough, but the tails only reached to midthigh and her socks to midcalf. There was far too much shapely leg exposed. He needed to find something to cover her. She made him remember things he wanted to forget. Yet he couldn't help but remember he'd been celibate a long time. His gaze moved over her silky skin. Too damn long.

When Ana finished the next batch, she placed them on the table. Jake speared two of the cakes and Ana took the others. Covering the stack with butter and syrup, she cut out a section, then forked a bite into her mouth.

Jake watched her eat in amazement. "The rain better stop or we'll run out of food."

"Oh, my," she gasped. "I never realized…I'm eating all your food."

He chuckled. "We have plenty. I went for supplies before the rain hit. We have enough staples for a few weeks. There's canned soups and stews, but the fresh bread and milk isn't going to last long."

Her chin came up. "I'll see that you're paid for everything I've used."

For some reason her wanting to pay made him angry. He hadn't done this for money. "You don't have to give me anything." His appetite suddenly gone, he got up from the table and dropped the last of his pancake into Max's bowl. This time, the dog eagerly ate what his master didn't want.

"You should be rewarded for what you did." Ana

stood, too. "You went out in this horrible weather and rescued me. I've invaded your home, even taken your bed."

Yeah, she was in his bed...but he wasn't. Stop thinking that way about her, he warned himself. "Don't worry about it," he called over his shoulder.

"I can't help it. I mean, we don't know how long this rain will continue."

"No one knows." He tried to shut out her soft voice with its proper British accent. Impossible. Since her arrival, the cabin had grown smaller by the minute, especially with her parading around in that damn shirt. He glanced at the fireplace, seeing her discarded skirt and jacket and skimpy silk underwear she'd washed out last night, and groaned at the memory of removing them from her body.

He sighed. He wasn't going to survive this.

"No one can look for me in this weather. This area is remote, you said so yourself. Who knows...I could be here indefinitely."

"Your plane more than likely had an ELT."

"What is that?"

"An Emergency Locater Transmitter. It sends out a signal so the authorities can find the plane. But this weather is bound to hold them up. To be honest, I didn't have time to look for it."

"What if it didn't have one?"

"Then we wait until the weather clears, I'll take you down the damn mountain myself."

She tilted her head, giving him an indignant look. "You don't have to get angry about it. I just don't want to be a burden."

Damn right she was a burden—to his peace of mind. He grabbed hold of her arm and swung her toward him. "You're not a burden, but you are frustrating as hell."

"You have no right to talk to me—"

Jake couldn't stop himself as he jerked her against him and covered her surprised mouth with his. He heard her startled gasp, but he didn't let up. When her lips parted, he took advantage and pushed his way inside.

Finally his common sense got the upper hand and he tore his mouth away. He saw her stunned face and felt like the world's biggest heel. "At least I know how to keep you quiet."

She slapped him across his face.

With the sting of Ana's hand still burning, he turned and walked out the door. The rain pelted him, drenching his clothes, but nothing could cool the fire inside him.

Chapter Four

"What do you mean you can't find any trace of the jet?"

At the Army command post on Penwyck, Colonel Pierceson Prescott faced Captain Millner who'd just relayed the report on the rescue efforts.

He didn't want to hear this. For the past four days, weather permitting, he'd sent out every search plane he could get his hands on to look for Royal Bird Two. As far as they could tell, the plane went down in a remote section of northern Wales.

"I'm sorry, colonel, but the weather has grounded all planes. Visibility is nonexistent."

Pierce knew all this, but he was head of Royal and Army Intelligence, for Christ's sake. An honored and decorated soldier. Even though he didn't use his title of duke, he'd earned it. He had accomplished many feats, gone beyond the call of duty time after time. But the worst task so far would be to go to Queen

Marissa and tell her they had to stop looking for her daughter.

He could tell by the look on the captain's face that there wasn't much hope that Anastasia had survived the crash. The last signal they'd gotten from the Lear jet had been over a rural area in the mountains in Wales. And dammit, the black box on the jet must have malfunctioned because they hadn't been able to pick up a signal.

"We will not give up the search. I gave my word to the queen—that means we'll keep looking until we find her, and by God, we will." He glared at the young officer, Jerrod Millner, as if daring him to say that the princess was dead.

How could he go to Meredith, the woman he loved more than life, and tell her there was no hope for her sister? He couldn't, not without exhausting every effort.

The colonel went to the large wall map and traced the northern section of Wales. "I want you to contact the authorities in this area, along with any farmers, hunters, anyone who knows that terrain and is willing to assist the SEALs. Go in on foot if you have to."

"But colonel, with the heavy rain, there's flooding."

"Bloody hell, captain, I've done recon exercise in worse conditions. We have to find her. What about the Royal Rangers? Could they jump in?"

He nodded. "A team has already volunteered and is standing by when the weather clears. We're doing everything possible to find Princess Anastasia."

"Make sure that you do, or you'll face the consequences." Pierce knew in his gut that he'd find the plane. But was he too late for the princess?

* * *

Thirty minutes later, Jake was calling himself a fool as he stood under the overhang of the small shed, listening to the rain sheet off the tin roof. The roughly built structure had two stalls and just enough extra room to store the feed for the two occupants, Toby and Maisie, a roan mare and a buckskin gelding he'd bought from the previous owner of the cabin.

Hell, the reason he'd bought this place was because he wanted to be alone. He needed time to think, to plan what to do about his future. Maybe he should just stay here for the remainder of his miserable life.

He'd known the second he found Ana that she'd come from wealth. Even with amnesia, her true personality showed through. She'd led a pampered life. Something he knew nothing about. Most of his life, he'd had to scratch and claw just to survive. Still, he didn't need to take it out on Ana.

Jake worked the grooming brush along Toby's flank, making the gelding's coat shine. The animal shifted against the aggressive treatment. Jake eased up.

"Sorry, boy. Didn't mean to take out my frustration on you."

Dammit, the woman had managed to get under his skin in little more than twenty-four hours. He should be in great shape after a few more days. Still, nothing had given him the right to pull a crazy stunt like kissing her. He was supposed to protect her, not attack her. He probably scared her to death. Good. Maybe that would keep her at a safe distance.

Toby whinnied and Jake looked over his shoulder to find Ana standing in the opening of the shed. She was wearing the oversized raincoat and a pair of his boots. The plastic bonnet should have looked silly, but on her it was appealing.

"You shouldn't be out here," he said. "It's cold."

"I'm warm enough. I found a pair of your sweatpants. I hope you don't mind that I borrowed them." She held up her palm. "Don't worry, I'm not going to say that I'll pay you. I'm just borrowing them. And since you're already upset, I must tell you I used some of your soap to wash up and your hairbrush, too."

"Look, Ana…about what happened…" He drew a breath. "I never should have…"

"Kissed me?" she finished.

He nodded. "It was uncalled for."

Ana didn't know what to think about this man. Memory or no memory, that kiss was like nothing she'd ever experienced before. Jake Sanderstone invoked feelings in her that felt new and exciting. "I'd say so."

She saw a flash of anger in his eyes, then hurried on to say, "Maybe I…I'm a little strong-willed."

He cocked an eyebrow. "Yeah, a little."

She shrugged, then looked around her surroundings. "It's going to be difficult to stay out of each other's way."

He turned back to Toby and continued the brushing. "I guess so."

"You said you need space. I take it that you aren't used to living with anyone."

"If you want to know if I'm married, the answer is no."

His answer was a relief to Ana. She came further into the shed and went over to the stall of a roan mare. She reached out and rubbed the mare's forehead. The animal responded to the attention. "You're a pretty girl,'' Ana said, then opened the gate, walked inside and reached for the currying brush. For the first time since she woke up yesterday, she felt like she had connected with something. Horses. In long sure strokes, she ran the brush over the animal's back.

''I take it you know your way around horses?''

She nodded. ''Maybe I have a horse of my own. What's her name?''

''Maisie.''

''Okay, Maisie.'' She smiled. ''Do you think you and I can be friends?''

For a while Jake and Ana continued grooming the horses, then Jake finally broke the silence, ''I want you to know that you don't have to worry about me doing anything like I did earlier.''

Ana stopped brushing. ''Which are you talking about? The way you yelled at me, or the kiss?''

''All of the above. I took my anger out on you. I had no right to manhandle you. It won't happen again.'' He looked at her, his eyes mesmerizing. ''You could be married...''

She couldn't imagine herself having a husband. If there were someone else, she doubted Jake's kiss would have caused such a reaction. ''I want to apologize for slapping you.'' Sudden emotions rose to her throat, but she swallowed them back. ''I don't like violence.''

He nodded. ''I provoked it.''

She doubted a man like Jake apologized much. ''It still wasn't right. And I'll try to stay out of your way.''

''Don't worry about it. I should have been more understanding of your situation. You're frightened and worried...''

"I'm not frightened," she said and realized she really wasn't, not with this man, her rescuer. "I'm upset over the deaths of the men in the plane. I'd hate to think I'm the cause."

"I told you you're not responsible. It was the weather or mechanical failure that caused the crash."

She glanced toward the rough terrain beyond the rocky ridge. "It seems so barbaric to leave them there all alone."

"There's nothing we can do now. Maybe when the weather clears, we can go back. Hopefully by then we'll have some help. And if your memory hasn't returned we might find some information about you." She nodded and for a while they were silent. He spoke first, "Again, I overstepped, Ana. It won't happen again. You have my word."

Ana wasn't surprised the man didn't once say the word "sorry." Most men had trouble admitting a mistake. Well, she wasn't going to let him off the hook so easily. "You're forgiven…if…"

He cocked an eyebrow. "What?"

"I'll forgive you, if you let me spend time out here taking care of Maisie and Toby."

He tossed her that cocky smile of his. "How generous of you."

"May I come out here?"

"Now let me understand this. You'd rather care for two smelly horses, feed them and muck out their stalls than cook inside a warm cabin."

"Yes," she said eagerly. "I think it might help with my memory, too. Perhaps when the weather clears we can go riding."

He raised a hand. "Now let's not get ahead of ourselves. I don't want you spending all your time out here. The weather…you could catch a cold."

"If you loan me some more clothes—"

"Lady, my wardrobe is pretty limited. Besides, we aren't exactly the same size."

Ana raised her chin. "I can understand if you don't trust me around your horses, but I assure you, I would never hurt them."

"I'm not worried about the damn horses, it's you. These guys are pretty gentle, but what if you get kicked or fall?" He frowned. "Just promise me you'll be careful."

She smiled. "I promise I'll be careful. And I'll be out of your way, too."

"Suits me." He came out of the stall and walked toward the cabin.

"Wait, we haven't finished our deal."

Jake stood just inside the overhang. "What?"

"I will feed horses and clean the stalls. But I want something, too."

He studied her for a moment, then finally said, "And what would that be?"

"That I won't have to cook."

She could tell that he didn't like being bested, but he hid his irritation well.

"It's a deal, but only if there are no complaints and you help with the dishes."

"That's unfair. I'll be doing more work…" She paused. "Okay, have it your way…this time. I'll get mine the next."

That's what worried him. "I have no doubt you will."

Sweat slithered down Jake's back as he crouched behind the Dumpster. Staring out into the pitch-black night, he couldn't see anything. But he knew one thing, Meg was inside the warehouse, unprotected. He didn't like that. He was going to give her two minutes to come out, or he would go in, and he didn't care if he was blowing their cover or not.

No more taking chances. If they lost the gun dealers or not, so be it, he wouldn't put Meg at risk any longer. That meant they had to get Novack tonight, or nearly two years of undercover work was down the drain.

A sound came from the warehouse and Jake alerted his backup that something was about to go down. Then Meg appeared in the doorway and his pulse leaped as she walked out with the known mercenary, Gil Novack, and two of his men.

"Come on, Meg. Just lead him to us," he muttered. From the beginning he hadn't wanted her to be the one to go in.

Suddenly the mood changed when Novack turned and said something to Meg. She looked shocked, then angry. With an unladylike gesture, Meg stormed off toward her car. What the hell had gone wrong?

Jake started to go after her, but another bureau agent grabbed him and held him back. Then before Jake could look back at his partner, an explosion rocked the ground and threw him backward.

"Meg! Meg!" he cried out as huge orange flames engulfed her car. Intense heat singed his body as he gulped needed air into his lungs, feeling the burning clear down to his stomach.

"Jake…Jake…" A soft voice spoke his name, then came a soothing hand against his damp skin. Still gasping for a breath, he opened his eyes to find Ana.

It was dark, only the light from the fire allowed him any sight. Her wavy hair circled around her face, her big eyes full of concern.

"What are you doing in here?" He tried to withdraw but she was sitting beside him on the couch, her hip tucked tight against his where he'd stretched out for the night. She had chosen one of his T-shirts to sleep in. He glanced down at her breasts, perfectly outlined by the thin cotton.

He bit back a groan and sat up.

"You cried out," she said. "I came in to see if you were all right." She touched him again. "You're shaking."

He sat up and moved to the end of the couch, but she was still too close. He glanced at the fire and found a makeshift clothesline with her lacy panties and bra drying next to his boxers. Short on clothes, she had to wash out the few things she had on a daily basis.

He groaned again. In only a few days, the woman had managed to crowd into practically every corner of his solitary life.

"You want to talk about it?" she asked. "The dream, I mean?"

Dream, hell, it was a nightmare. "No. I do not want to talk about it."

"Maybe you'll feel better."

He gave her a sideways glance. "It amazes me how women think that if you just talk about it, it'll make it better. Well, I got news for you, chère, nothing will make this better." He stood, grabbed his shirt off the table and jerked his arms into the sleeves as he crossed the room to the farthest corner.

For a long time there was only the crackling sound of the fire.

"I'm sorry," Ana sighed. "I only wanted to help. When you cried out…I thought you needed…I mean, you've been taking care of me and I only wanted to return the favor."

"I don't need any favors."

"I'm sorry to hear that," she said in a whispered voice.

There was long silence, then Ana's soft footsteps as she headed back to the bedroom. Good. He didn't want to rehash any of this. He raked a shaky hand through his hair. His past was his business. But the thought of being alone right now was worse.

"I worked for the FBI," he began.

More silence, then Ana spoke, "That sounds like a dangerous occupation."

He glanced over his shoulder at her. Mistake. She looked like an angel, but he definitely wasn't having angelic thoughts about her. He hadn't since the moment he'd laid eyes on her. All that honey-colored hair laying in waves against her delicate shoulders. His T-shirt nearly swallowed her up, but didn't hide the curves, her full breasts and shapely hips. He drew a labored breath. He'd always been a leg man.

He shifted his thoughts away. "My particular job was dangerous. I was on a two-year undercover assignment."

"I take it you're no longer undercover. I understand your FBI doesn't work outside the United States."

Another piece of her memory. Did she work for the Penwyck government? He had to get back to the crash site. There were too many unanswered questions.

"Not that they advertise about, and no, I'm not on any assignment. I no longer work for the bureau."

"I imagine you were good at your job," she said and started across the room toward him.

Jake tensed. He didn't need her to come any closer. He was too vulnerable right now. He ached for nothing more than to hear her whispered comfort, to feel her gentle touches and make him forget…to erase the nightmares. He just didn't deserve them. Not after what he'd done. He had to push Ana away….

"Yeah, chère, I was so good that I was responsible for my partner's death." Seeing the shocked look on her face, he knew he'd hit his target. He grabbed a raincoat off the hook, slipped it on, then walked out the door.

When the latch clicked shut, Ana sank against the back of the couch. That explains a lot, she thought. She looked at Max, standing by the door.

Jake's moods, his brooding, the sadness in his eyes. Her heart went out to the man who had rescued her. And by her own admission, she hadn't been the most gracious houseguest. She seemed to have a knack for irritating him, remembering the kiss they'd shared, even if it was in anger. Just the thought that he'd desired her, sent a thrill through her. Jake Sanderstone had a skilled mouth and knew how to use it.

These feelings had kept Ana awake the past two nights. But Jake obviously hadn't felt the same, he been doing everything to stay away from her. He'd acted as if she had the plague. When she heard him cry out in his sleep, she came running, wanting to help him. But once he saw it was her, he couldn't get far enough away. That hurt. Then she learned the heavy burden he'd been carrying around. Now, she understood so much. He'd been living here for months, alone, brooding over what happened.

She knew what it felt like to feel you'd caused someone's death. Her thoughts turned to the men in the plane. Had she been responsible for their fate?

In the past few days, she'd gotten to know Jake Sanderstone. This man couldn't have been responsible for his partner's death. But nothing would change until Jake believed that, too.

At dawn, Ana forced herself out of bed. Tired, she suspected she'd never been an early riser. Pulling on sweatpants and a flannel shirt to protect her against the cold, she went to tend to her chore, the horses.

In the main room of the cabin, she found Jake asleep on the couch. So as not to disturb him, she tiptoed past him to the sink. She had overstepped the line last night, and she didn't want a repeat confrontation first thing in the morning.

She quietly pumped enough water to brush her teeth. Jake had given her one of his extra toothbrushes. After finishing the task, she placed the toothbrush back in the glass next to his. Pushing aside her awareness of the intimacy of that simple act, she turned to the cupboard and reached for a can of juice. Grabbing her rain gear, she went out to the porch.

She spent the next hour in the shed, mucking out the stalls and grooming Maisie and Toby, wishing she could exercise the restless animals.

"I know how you feel," she said aloud, watching the steady stream of rain running off the structure. Just a repeat of the four days before. Her thoughts turned to Jake, knowing he must be going crazy, too.

She spent more time in the shed to avoid the confines of the small cabin. After cleaning up and polishing some tack, she was rewarded with a nice find. An old pair of canvas shoes. Finished with the chores, Ana walked back to the cabin, allowing the rain to wash over her. Her heavy rain wear pretty much kept her dry, but she needed the freedom of the open space. By the time she reached the porch she was chilled, but didn't care.

When she walked in, she found Jake at the stove cooking breakfast. She couldn't help but stop and enjoy the view. Jake Sanderstone was too good to pass up. In a pair of old jeans, he was lethal. His bottom was firm, his thighs toned. Her gaze slid upward to his narrow waist, then higher to the expanse of his muscular back and broad shoulders. Her pulse began to race, her breathing became difficult.

He was perfection.

Suddenly he turned toward her and her cheeks flamed. He frowned. "Are you all right?"

She nodded, unable to speak. Turning around, she hung up her coat and took off her boots. Then picking up her find in the barn she walked to the table.

"Look," she said in a throaty voice. "I found them in the shed." She held up a ratty pair of old shoes. "May I borrow them?"

Jake blinked at the once-white tennis shoes and nearly laughed. What woman would care so much about shoes that should be in the trash? He was beginning to realize that his survivor was far from ordinary. "I don't care. I don't think anyone is going to fight you for them."

"Well, I didn't know if they belonged to someone you know, someone who'd been up here...for a visit."

So she was wondering about a woman. That intrigued him. It also made him think about how long it'd been since he'd…shared company with a woman. Or even wanted to until… "I haven't had any visitors," he grumbled.

"Oh, then I guess they were left behind by the previous tenant."

"Must have been."

"Good, then I won't wear out your socks." Smiling, she sat down and pulled them on.

"I have plenty of socks. But those are the only sweats I have. You wear those out, you're in trouble." He was the one in trouble. For his own sanity, he needed to keep Ana covered.

"All I know is that my feet are covered. She stood and they both glanced down at the too big, at least by a whole size, shoes. She had to lace them tight just to keep them on her feet.

He bit back a grin as he placed the plate in front of her. "Sit, and eat your eggs," he ordered.

"What kind of eggs are these?"

"Scrambled. I broke the yolks."

She wrinkled her nose and sank into her chair. "They're mixed together."

"Is that a problem?" he asked. "You can wear old shoes, but you can't eat your eggs scrambled, chère?"

"Don't call me…" she stopped. "Of course I can eat them. I just don't like—remember ever having eggs this way."

Dammit, he was goading her again. He released a long sigh and sat down across from her. "Just try them. A lot of people prefer them this way."

She added a little salt, then picked up her fork and took a bite. "They are good."

"I mixed in a little canned ham. Enjoy them, because that's the last of them. From now on, we'll be eating pancakes."

"Until the rain stops," she said optimistically.

Jake took a bite of his food, then glanced toward the window. "Hard to tell when that will be. It's been four days since I've seen blue sky."

"It would be nice to go outside without getting wet." She looked at him. "Jake, I know my being here has been hard on you. I mean, you have no privacy…"

"We've managed," he lied. He didn't tell her what just being in the same room with her did to his libido. How she made him think about things he could never have.

Dressed in his clothes and those too-big shoes, she was one class act. Even if he was looking—which he wasn't—a woman like Ana was out of his league. In so many ways. There was no doubt in his mind that Ana had a man waiting for her return. A man better suited, to her, one who knew how to treat her.

Once she was safely back with her family, he could move on with his life.

"When you get home, you'll be able to push these miserable days from your memory."

Ana rested her fork on the plate. "I doubt I ever will. There are two men over the ridge who died in the crash I survived." Sadness clouded her pretty face. "I can't stand the fact they're up there… exposed."

"There wasn't anything I could do," he said, trying to keep his frustration from his voice. "They were already dead and you were alive, Ana, and I needed to keep you that way."

She nodded and began to rub her temples. "I just wish...I could remember something. This is so maddening not knowing...."

"I'd say it's a good thing," he began.

"The hell it is," she spat out.

Taken aback by her sudden burst of anger, he hid a smile. "I know it's frustrating, Ana, but your memory loss could just be your way of shutting out the trauma."

"I can understand that, but why can't I at least remember my name? My family?"

"A husband?" he asked.

She looked at him with those brilliant sapphire eyes and he felt his chest tighten.

"There isn't a husband or any man."

His eyes bore into hers. "Have you looked in the mirror? You have a man."

She shook her head, not letting go of his gaze. "Not one I want. I know I would remember someone special," she insisted as her cheeks turned rosy, then her voice lowered, "or your kiss wouldn't have mattered."

With a mumbled curse, Jake looked away. He didn't need to hear this. "I told you I was trying to—"

"Shut me up," she finished for him.

They sat there staring, then finally Jake said, "You're a beautiful woman, I don't deny that. And hell, I'm only human. But you have my word, Ana, I won't touch you again. You are safe with me as long as you are on this mountain."

"A girl can't ask for more than that." She stood and walked off toward the bedroom. When the door closed, Jake released a long breath. He was in trouble.... Big trouble.

Between his sleepless nights and her crowding his days, he couldn't even think straight anymore. Hell, at the bureau, they had called him "the ice man." He was a champion at freezing people out. He'd found the only way to keep sane, to keep from getting hurt was to never allow anyone to get close. Especially a woman.

What he hadn't figured on was someone like Ana coming into his life. He couldn't get involved with her. Hell, she didn't even know who she was. He did. She was a beautiful woman, who if he allowed it, would steal his heart. He would keep her safe as he promised. But how could he protect himself?

Chapter Five

Two mornings later, Ana climbed out of bed and slipped on her sweats and flannel shirt. She walked into the main room of the cabin and found Jake stretched out on the couch, asleep. Or was he? She expected that with his training, the man was alert to every noise. It was so tempting to lean down closer to see for sure. But the fear that he might throw her to the floor warned her off the idea.

To avoid her, he'd wait until she left the cabin before he got up and started breakfast. Past evenings, he busied himself with reading one of his many paperbacks or went on the porch to play with his knife and some scrap of wood.

She usually retired to the bedroom early. She would hate to be responsible for his freezing to death. There were other ways to torture him. If only she were brave enough to carry them off.

She put on her rainwear and boots as usual, then

opened the door. A surprise awaited her as she stood in the doorway and looked out.

"Close the damn door, you're letting in the cold air," Jake called from the couch.

"Oh, my God," Ana whispered. "Jake, come out here. Look."

"I'll look later. Just shut the damn door," he yelled and rolled over.

"Well, then you're going to miss it," she announced. Stripping off her raincoat, she stepped off the porch onto the soggy earth.

The rain had stopped.

She grinned and ran around in her too-big boots. It was still overcast, but for now, there wasn't any rain.

Brushing his blanket aside, Jake stood up wearing his usual sleep attire these days, jeans. He made his way to the door to discover it had stopped raining. He also caught sight of Ana dancing in the front yard. Seeing her antics, he had a feeling she was that way with life, too. He envied her that. To be free, so eager for every day to begin that you smiled just getting out of bed. He couldn't ever remember feeling that way.

"Hey, don't you have chores to do?" he called to her.

"Not until I finish celebrating this glorious day. Come out here and breathe in this beautiful clear morning."

"I'd rather have another hour of sleep." He turned away from her tempting body, then before he could close the door, felt a pebble bounce off his back. Then came her giggle.

He turned around, Ana's smile was a defiant challenge. She looked like a sprite. "You're going to get it now," he said. Shirtless and barefoot, he stepped off the porch and went after her.

Excitement raced through Ana as she managed to elude him, but she expected it was only because he let her. With his agile body, he moved easily around the terrain until finally he trapped her beside a tall pine.

She squealed as he captured her. Ana felt even more excitement as his arms went around her, bringing her close against him. Then to her shock, he swung her up and over his shoulder.

"Jake, put me down," she cried, feeling his large hand on her leg.

"You shouldn't have thrown rocks at me," he said. "Now, you must pay."

"It was only one, and it was a pebble. Please, I need to feed Toby and Maisie."

"The horses can wait, you must be punished."

Max joined in the romp and danced around them barking. Jake showed off his athletic abilities as he crouched down to pick up a small branch and toss it for the dog.

"Max, help me," Ana called. "Jake, what are you going to do?"

"Make sure you pay for your sins." He walked over to the big metal tub filled with water on the porch, prepared to drop her into it, but she clung to him.

"Jake, you wouldn't dare."

"Wouldn't I?"

"Please, Jake don't," she cried, enjoying the feel of his bare skin under her hands. "I'll do anything."

"Now this could get interesting. Will you do the dishes?"

"All right, I'll do the dishes," she said grudgingly.

He righted her, then set her down. At first a little unsteady, she swayed against him.

"Whoa, there," he said, gripping her by the arms. "You okay?"

She drew a breath and his scent filled her nostrils. She managed to nod as he continued to hold on to her. "Just a little dizzy," she said.

"Damn, I shouldn't have been so rough."

"You weren't rough. The blood just rushed to my head. It happens when you're turned upside down."

He smiled. "And just how do you know that?"

"I don't know. I took a first-aid course. It was required…" Her eyes grew wide and she frowned.

He nodded. "Go on.

"Oh, Jake. I remembered."

"And more will come."

She looked at him. "I like you this way. It makes me feel good."

He wanted to close up and pull back, but she was right, he didn't need to take his frustrations out on her. "I've never been good company."

"I wouldn't say that." She folded her arms. "But a little more than grunting sounds would be nice. So what will we do today? We can't let this good weather go to waste. Is it too much to hope that the road is drivable?"

"It'll take more than a few hours to dry out." Jake found he wanted to find something to keep her smiling. He glanced up at the sky. "While we're getting a break in the weather, why don't we go fishing?"

"Oh, Jake, really?"

"Really," he agreed. "You go feed Maisie and Toby and I'll gather up the gear." He turned her in the direction of the shed and gave her a gentle shove. To his surprise, he was looking forward to spending the morning with her. He pushed aside the feeling that it wasn't a good idea.

If Jake had his way, he'd go up to the lake, but that was a two-mile hike and he wasn't sure how the weather, or Ana, would hold out. So he chose the stream not far from the cabin.

"Do you think we'll catch anything?" she asked.

"Not sure." He helped her over the rocky bank, found a large rock and spread out the blanket. He had her sit beside him. "Do you remember ever fishing?"

"No." She took hold of the pole he offered.

"I guess you want me to bait the hook."

"I wouldn't mind if you did, the first time anyway."

He opened the jar of moist earth and dug out a worm. He was surprised when she didn't act squeamish as he pushed the sharp hook through the creature. Finished, he tossed her line into the water.

"What do I do now?" she asked.

"Just hang on."

"Okay." She gripped the pole tightly.

"Ease up a little, this is supposed to be fun."

"I just don't want my fish to get away."

He noticed her serious expression and he couldn't help but smile. "So you think you're going to catch a fish?"

"Of course. And you're going to cook it." She scooted to the edge of the rock and looked down into the rushing stream.

"I hate to disappoint you, but some days I come

back empty-handed. And I'm a Louisiana boy. I could dangle a pole in the water before I could walk.''

"That's impressive, but I plan to catch dinner for us.''

"Sounds like a challenge.''

"Maybe.'' She studied her fishing line.

"Then let's make this interesting.''

"Very well. If I catch the first fish, you not only cook it, but do the dishes, too.''

He smiled again. "You're too easy, chère. And if I catch the first fish?''

"I'll cook you breakfast tomorrow.''

"I'm not sure that's a winning deal.'' Then he felt her sharp elbow land hard against his ribs. "Hey, that hurt.''

"Well, you deserved it. I've never said bad things about your cooking.''

"That's because I'm a pretty good cook.''

Ana arched a quizzical brow. "Oh, really?''

"Let's just say nothing has stopped you from eating.''

Ana's eyes flared and her sweet bow-shaped mouth opened. He wanted nothing more than to kiss her again. Losing the battle for control, he leaned closer and was about to cover her mouth when she gasped and turned away.

"My line,'' she cried. "Something tugged on my line.''

Jake couldn't believe it. "A fish.''

She pulled up on the pole. "Hurry. What do I do?''

"If I didn't want fish for dinner so badly, I'd let you figure it out yourself.'' He reached for her line and tugged the fish out of the water.

"Not you, Jake Sanderstone. You're too nice a guy."

He turned and sent her a scorching glance. "Don't be too sure of that."

They ended up with three fish, not huge, but enough for a nice meal. Ana had caught two of them; nothing about the woman surprised Jake anymore. He could tell she'd spent time in the outdoors. She was steady on the trail and small rodents and forest animals hadn't bothered her as they hiked the long way back to the cabin. He still didn't want to tempt fate with those threatening clouds overhead.

Then together they sat on the porch and cleaned the catch for dinner. They talked about the area, and places that Jake had traveled over the years. She was careful not to bring up anything from his years with the bureau. He realized he'd enjoyed spending the day with her.

"How are you going to cook the fish?"

"I'm going to pan fry them with salt and pepper. I have some rice we can cook up."

"What's this *we* business?" she asked with an attempt at innocent. "I thought you were in charge of the cooking tonight."

"I thought I'd help with Maisie and Toby and you'd help me cook." He carried the fish inside.

She followed him. "Well, since you asked so nicely," she said sarcastically.

He put the fillets on the counter. "You're not giving an inch, are you?"

She placed her hands on her hips. "Just hours ago, you held me upside down and threatened to drop me into a rain barrel."

He stood in front of her. "After you threw a rock at me."

"A pebble."

"You could have hit my head and hurt me."

"Such whining. You sound like my sisters…" Her hand went to her mouth. "Oh, my, Lord. I said I have sisters."

Jake watched as her eyes filled with tears. "Now stay calm. Let it happen. Do you remember their names?"

Looking dazed, she shook her head. "Oh, this is so frustrating." Her hands fisted at her sides.

"Just slow down. There's a lot to dredge up. Go take a rest and I'll handle things here."

She looked up at him. "But…I was going to help."

"There's no need. You've done plenty of things around here. Maisie and Toby have never had so much attention."

"I enjoy it."

"Well, it won't hurt you to rest awhile. I hear you moving around in the middle of the night."

"I don't mean to disturb you."

Too late. She already had. "I know, but we've been stuck inside for too long. Hopefully, the rain has stopped for a while."

"Then we can go down the mountain?"

"The road needs to dry out for a few days. It's still too muddy. If we're lucky the weather might hold until then." He doubted it. "Now, go lie down and take a nap."

"I sleep too much during the day."

"Go on. I don't need you in my way," he said and shoved her toward the bedroom. "I'll wake you in an hour."

"I won't be able to sleep," she called from the doorway.

Jake shook his head, then went to work. Looking into the cupboard, he found a bag of rice and two cans of vegetables. Green beans or peas. Did Ana like peas? He walked to the bedroom and started to ask, but stopped when he found her sound asleep.

He went to the bed, removed her shoes and pulled the blanket over her. Unable to resist, he brushed strands of hair from her face. The hike must have worn her out. He wished it had done the same for him. His body stiffened with tension. He hadn't had a good night's sleep since she had arrived.

Now, he found himself wondering what he was going to do when she was gone.

The table was set for dinner.

Jake even had napkins tucked under the knife and spoon at both place settings. It was far from fancy, and he'd bet Ana had had better, but it was the best he could do. The vegetables were warmed and the coffee ready to be poured. At the stove, the fresh fish simmered in a cast-iron skillet. His mouth watered as the incredible aroma teased his nostrils. It was surprising what butter and a little lemon pepper seasoning could do for trout.

He couldn't help but wonder if Ana would like it. What a joke. In the past, he'd never cared much about pleasing anyone. At the bureau, he'd been the "loner" because he never depended on anyone. Undercover assignments had been best for him. That way Jake got to play everyone else but himself. The only one he'd let get close was his partner Meg, but unlike her, he'd lived to regret it.

Ana was different. She could make a man forget to think, only feel. All his life he'd fought attachments. His own mother hadn't wanted him. He wasn't cut out to be the loving family man. But couldn't rid his mind of thoughts of Ana and her rich blue eyes, her inviting mouth.

A crackling sound drew his attention to the fish. Seeing his meal was about to be ruined, he grabbed the skillet handle without thinking, burning his hand on the hot metal. He cursed loudly, then used the pot holder to remove the pan from the burner.

He sucked in a breath as he looked down at the long red welt across his palm. Careful of his injury, he used his other hand to prime the pump, letting the cool water run over the wound. That's when Ana appeared at his side.

"What happened?" she cried.

He withdrew his throbbing hand and held it up.

"Oh, Jake. It must hurt."

"Like hell."

Ana looked up at him, her eyes reflecting her concern. "I'll get some antiseptic cream from the kit," she said, then busied herself searching through the small box.

"I can do it." He didn't need a nurse. He could take care of himself.

She returned to him with a tube of cream. "Sit down," she prompted and pointed to the chair.

Jake wanted to tell her to leave him alone. He never liked being babied, but found himself doing as she asked. He straddled the chair and held out his hand.

"It's just a burn. I'm more worried about the fish."

"I don't care about dinner. Making sure this wound doesn't get infected is more important." She took his hand in hers and squeezed out some cream. Then she gently smoothed it over the injured skin.

Jake's hands were much larger than hers. He was a big man, and strong. He had easily picked her up this morning, and she'd liked the way he made her feel. Protected. She like their differences. The sandpaper roughness of his skin against her smooth skin.

His breathing abruptly changed.

"Am I hurting you?"

He closed his eyes, and shook his head. "No. It feels…okay."

Ana studied his face, his square jaw, straight nose and deep-set eyes. He wasn't classically handsome, not with his brooding manner, but his strong presence made him more than appealing.

Her gaze moved to his furrowed brow and she fought the urge to stroke it. "Good."

Jake opened his eyes and heat surged through her. How dangerously close they were. Then came a flashback to earlier at the stream when Jake almost kissed her. Even now, she wanted it so badly, but terrified he would reject her so she moved back. She took the bandage and wrapped the gauze strip around the palm.

"I…you don't want to get an infection."

"That's the least of my worries." He pulled his hand away and finished doing the job. "This burn isn't so bad. I've had a lot worse."

He turned back to the stove and retrieved the skillet from the stove. "Have a seat. I promised to fix you dinner."

"But your hand…"

"It's fine." He brought the fish to the table, then

went back for the vegetables. He poured them both coffee and looked up with a frown. "Take your seat."

Knowing better than to argue, Ana sank into her chair. She picked up her napkin and placed it over her lap. "This smells delicious."

"That's because it is. I know how to fry fish. Even under the crudest of conditions."

He passed her the platter and Ana took one of the fillets, wishing she still had an appetite. She added vegetables and a piece of bread to her plate.

"This is good," she said after her first bite.
He didn't say a word. He just gave her an "I told you so" smirk.

Ana continued to eat, but the conversation was pretty one-sided. She was the only one talking. What had happened? They been getting along all day, then suddenly it changed. "Jake, did I do something to offend you?"

Finished, he rocked back in his chair and sipped his coffee. "Why do you say that?"

"You're so quiet."

"I usually am when I don't have anything to say."

"You didn't seem to have any trouble talking to me while we were fishing and even up until I went to lie down."

Jake let the legs of his chair drop back to the floor, then he leaned toward her. "Stop playing games, Ana."

"Then you stop playing them." She stood. "Common courtesy would be to acknowledge that I was in the room."

"Dammit woman, I'm trying my best to be a gentleman by keeping my distance."

She swallowed hard, and raised her chin. "I didn't ask you to."

His eyes grew dark and dangerous. "Don't play with fire, chère, you'll only get burned." He stood, then walked to the door. "I'll do the dishes later."

"Jake," she called after him, then went to the door. "Don't go."

His shoulders tensed.

"I'm tired of being alone," she said, hating herself for sounding needy. "Day after day, you leave me. Until today. Is my company so…difficult?"

"It's the way I am," he said tensely, raking fingers through his hair. "I don't do well with people."

"No, that's not true," she disagreed. "You allowed yourself to have fun today. I got to know the real you, without the walls." She could see she wasn't getting through to him. "But when you leave me…or ignore the fact that I'm around." She swallowed hard. "Sometimes…I wish…you would had left me on the mountain."

He stared at her. "Don't you understand, Ana? I'm trying to do the right thing. You have a life somewhere else. When you leave here, I don't want you to have…regrets."

"I already have regrets, Jake. I regret that two men died in the crash. I regret that I don't remember who I am. But I will *never* regret anything we share during our time together." Her breathing grew ragged. She was so angry she wanted to cry. "Maybe you're the one with regrets, Jake, not me."

She stepped past him and reached for her coat, then the doorknob. "You stay here this time, I'll leave. I refuse to drive you out of your home again." She marched out the door, without a clue as to where she was going.

And, she didn't care.

This was the only place she felt like she belonged. Ana found her way to the shed with Maisie and Toby. She might not have much memory of who she was, but she knew she must have had animals in her life. Horses. She knew the name of every piece of tack. How to brush and care for Toby and Maisie.

She had a strange feeling that something terrible had happened in her past, and it had been the companionship of her horse that had gotten her through it. She closed her eyes and could almost feel the powerful beast beneath her as she raced through lush green pasture. She'd loved the feel of the breeze against her face and the freedom....

Slowly her smile faded. That was a dream. Known fact; she was on a mountain top in Wales, without a memory of a blasted thing. And Jake Sanderstone didn't want her here. Why would he? She'd invaded his home. Maybe if she weren't so attracted to him, she wouldn't be so hurt by his rejection tonight.

But earlier they'd been so happy. He'd been enjoying himself as much as she had. And she also knew that he was attracted to her, too. Even though she smelled of horses, her face hadn't seen makeup in nearly a week and she hadn't had a real bath in as long.

She moaned. What she wouldn't give for a long hot bath with her favorite jasmine bath salts. She closed her eyes and could feel the water, smell the flowery scent. She gasped and opened her eyes. She remembered something. A large tiled bathroom with an enormous raised tub filled with mounds of bubbles. It wasn't much. If only she could see a person. Outside of feeling she had sisters, Ana couldn't remember anything about her life, not a man or a close friend, not even parents.

"Ana…"

She swung around to find Jake standing at the edge of the shed.

"Please, can we talk?"

"I think we both said enough," she said.

He shook his head. "No, I need to say…I'm sorry. You're right, I treated you badly."

Even now, Jake still had to fight the urge to reach for her. And each day, it grew more and more difficult to stay away. "I've been taking out my frustrations on you."

"I know I'm crowding you…and if I could…I would leave." Her lower lip trembled. "Maybe if the weather is clear tomorrow, you can take me down the mountain."

Jake moved toward her, knowing he was treading on dangerous ground. He was getting too close, but he needed to touch Ana, to hold her. It had been so long since he'd had human contact. Extending his hand, he reached for her, tugged and she came into his arms. Paradise. There was no other word to describe the feel of her body against his.

"I don't want you to go, chère. If it were up to me, you would never…" He stopped himself before he said too much.

She raised her head, her blue eyes filled with hope. "You want me to stay?"

"I don't have any right to want anything."

"You have every right, Jake," she said. "I told

you before there isn't a man in my life.'' Her hands moved up his chest. "There can't be. Not when I am having these feelings about you. And don't try to act indifferent to me. Not when your heart is pounding like a drum.'' She gently cupped his bandaged hand and kissed it, then placed it over her heart. He lost all capability to breathe, feeling her full breast against his fingers.

"I don't want to leave you,'' she confessed.

If he didn't back off now, it would be too late. Ana wasn't his to take, and it would be worse to hope, then later lose her anyway. He pulled back. "We have to stop this, Ana. We need to think about what we're doing. Please.''

"Jake, why are you denying what you feel?''

He could almost taste her, her lips were just inches from his. "Because we can't allow anything to happen.''

"Just a kiss… Just one.''

He couldn't turn her down. How could one kiss hurt? That was what he told himself, but when his lips touched hers, he knew that one would never be enough.

Ana had never experienced anything like Jake's kiss. His masterful mouth coaxed and teased hers, filling her with a need that made her body throb. His arms tightened, pulling her against his body, leaving no doubt that he desired her.

Ana reached up and raked her hands through his hair at the nape. Her breasts flattened against his chest, adrenaline pulsing through her body as his tongue pushed into her mouth, tasting, stroking, greedily demanding more. Her breasts grew heavy and her nipples tingled as the new sensations rushed over her, frustration, hunger, and other cravings she couldn't name. She twisted closer, and he groaned deep in his throat.

Then Jake suddenly broke away. His eyes still smoldered with desire, but she also saw his regret.

"Dammit, Ana," he rasped out, his features drawn tight as he gazed at her mouth. "This is a mistake. It wouldn't be right." He turned and rushed off into the night.

Ana watched as he walked away from the cabin into the woods. She glanced down at the dog. "Go with him, Max. He needs you." The animal didn't hesitate and took off after his master.

Ana wanted to cry. Once again, she was alone.

Chapter Six

Ana rolled over in bed and snuggled deeper under the blanket to fight off the cold. She opened her eyes to see it was still dark outside. Good, she could sleep a little longer. She curled up for warmth and started to drift off again when an annoying rhythmic noise wouldn't stop. It almost sounded like…rain.

She jerked up, climbed to her knees on the mattress and looked out the window over the bed. Pulling back the musty curtains, she found a depressing sight, a virtual downpour going on outside.

"No," she cried. "This can't be." The rain was so heavy, it streamed down the window.

Suddenly the door opened and Jake appeared. Shirtless, his hair was mussed and his eyes filled with sleep. He looked so…irresistible.

"What's the matter?" he asked, rubbing his hand over his stubbled jaw.

"It's raining."

He gave a glance toward the window. "I see that. But you should be used to that."

"Well, it's becoming tiresome." Her fists clenched. "I thought I'd be leaving today...."

He shrugged. "Well, I guess not. Looks like you're stuck here for a while longer." He started to walk out, making Ana even more furious. How dare he dismiss her like that?

Ana scrambled off the bed and went after him. "Wait just one minute, Jake Sanderstone."

He paused, then slowly turned around and tossed her a stern look. She swallowed back her nervousness. She wasn't going to let this man intimidate her any longer. No matter how wonderfully he'd kissed her. A remembered warmth spread through her body as she relived their encounter in the shed. She was already angry that it had cost her a sleepless night.

"Is there something you want?"

You, she thought. "Yes, there is. I know your patience is wearing thin, but you need not behave like...like it's my fault. We're grown adults, we should be able to be cordial to each other."

His eyes took on a challenging glint. They turned dark and serious. "Being cordial is the last thing on my mind, chère. Not after that kiss."

More heat pulsed through her body. "I thought... you wanted to forget about it," she said, fighting to control her breathing.

"Hell, I want to forget a lot of things." He ran his hand over his face, the bandage still covering his burned palm. "Can we not discuss this?"

She folded her arms, trying to fight the blush to her cheeks. "You're the one who brought it up in the first place. We should find a way to deal with it."

"There's *no* dealing with it," he snapped, "because we're going to forget it ever happened."

That hurt, but Ana wasn't going to let him see it. "Fine, we'll forget it happened as long as you at least make an effort to be civil." She took a breath. "Like it or not, I'm here until you take me down the mountain, or someone comes for me."

"I know that better than anyone," he said. "Is that all?"

"Yes, I believe so," she said. "Now, if you'll excuse me, I'll get dressed and go feed Toby and Maisie." She glanced down at her bare legs, then looked up at Jake to see him staring at her. Suddenly it felt as if he could see through her shirt. With a tilt of her head, she pivoted and walked to the bedroom.

Jake was tempted, but this wasn't a joke. He was attracted to Ana. Big time. Damn. That kiss was another huge mistake. He never should have touched her. What was he going to do about it? He knew what he wanted to do, but he had to control that impulse.

Even if he were looking for a relationship, Ana wasn't his type. Besides, even with no memory, she had commitment written all over her. Just knowing that, he should turn and run the other way. But he couldn't, they were stuck. Together.

At that moment he decided, just as soon as the rain stopped, he was going back to the crash site. There were answers there, somewhere. There had to be more clues, more information on the pilot. Why was a Black Knight flying that plane? The big question was what was Ana doing with him?

Jake wanted to believe she was an innocent bystander, but he'd come from a world in which everybody had an angle. People used people to get what they wanted, to survive. He hadn't trusted anyone in a very long time, and a woman… Forget it. As a young boy, trust had been a luxury. The only person he'd been able to depend on was himself. His father had taken off long before Jake's birth. Even as a boy, Jake had been his mother's caretaker.

No, he wasn't very trusting when it came to people, but he'd learned how to avoid getting hurt. Just so long as he kept his distance from Ana. He'd let her get far too close last night. Somehow he had to wait this out, then when he got her off the mountain he could go back to normal. He'd been content for months before Ana's arrival, he could be content again. That's what he had to keep telling himself. Maybe he'd even start to believe it.

Ana finished her chores quickly. Feeding the horses and cleaning out their stalls was all she could handle today. She wasn't in a good mood. Spending time in the shed only reminded her of Jake's rejection. So she decided to spend the rest of the day in the bedroom, reading. She'd avoid Jake Sanderstone. That didn't mean she wasn't going to think about him. She hated it, but that was exactly what would happen, she'd relive the kiss again and again. Great. How pathetic could a person be?

She ran back through the heavy rain and onto the porch. She shook off most of the water then opened the cabin door. After hanging up her coat, she stepped out of her boots and turned around to find Jake at the stove.

He looked over his shoulder and smiled. "Have a seat, breakfast is nearly ready." He held out a cup of coffee.

Surprised at his change of attitude, she decided not to mention it. "Thank you." She took the mug and their fingers brushed. A charge surged through her, but with effort she only smiled.

"You hungry?" he asked.

Suddenly she was. "Famished."

"Good. I'm making pancakes."

Her mouth watered. She hadn't eaten much last night. "Sounds good. Do you need some help?"

He shook his head. "No, just sit down. You did enough chores already this morning."

She took a sip of her coffee and slid into her chair. "I hear that you're a good cook."

"That's what they say." He scooped up the cakes, then moved the griddle from the burner. He brought the stack to the table. "But, I'd rather have my guest tell me." He pulled out the other chair. He offered her the platter. After she took two, he stabbed the remaining cakes. "I can make more."

"I don't want you to use up all your cake mix on me."

He shrugged. "I can get more." He poured syrup over the stack.

She placed the napkin across her lap.

"You know, you do that every time."

"Do what?"

"Put the napkin on your lap," he said pointing. "It's like second nature to you. And the way you speak and handle yourself shows me that you're educated. Either that, or you've gone to one of those finishing schools."

"I believe it's common practice to use a napkin."

"Of course, but with you, it's also the way you do things. The way you hold your fork and knife." His gaze raised to meet hers. "That suit you were wearing when I found you had a designer label. Maybe you worked for the Penwyck government."

Ana took a bite and after swallowing she said, "Are we playing guess my occupation?"

"Sure beats sitting around with nothing to do." He shoved a forkful of pancakes into his mouth.

"Why don't we talk about you?"

He shook his head. "I'm not very interesting."

She cut another wedge out of the stack. "You were with the FBI. I wouldn't say that's dull."

Jake stiffened. It hadn't been. His job had been deadly serious. "I had top secret clearance. There are a lot things I still can't talk about." Jake didn't like where this was going. "Why don't we change the topic of conversation to something else."

"Like the weather?"

They both laughed. Suddenly the gloom lifted, and Ana smiled. She was a beautiful woman, and she stirred feelings in him that had been dormant for a long time.

"I know it's been pretty miserable here for you, and I haven't helped."

"It's understandable. You came up here to be alone...and all of a sudden I showed up."

"It hasn't been that bad." He found he liked talking with her. "I wish I could have gotten you down the mountain. Your family has to be worried sick."

She frowned. "I suppose. I don't mean to sound heartless, but when you have no memory of any-one...it's hard to miss them." She looked so sad, then she blinked and smiled. "What about your family?"

"There was just my mother and me. She's been

gone a long time. In my line of work, a family man isn't best suited for the undercover jobs.''

"You never wanted a family? Children?''

Jake wanted a lot of things, including the woman across from him, but that didn't mean he'd ever get it. "I doubt I'd make a good father. I didn't have much of an example.''

She sighed thoughtfully. "I want children.''

Jake watched her face light up. "You'd be a good mother,'' he said, not realizing he'd spoken out loud.

She gave him a surprised look. "How would you know?''

"I've seen you with Toby and Maisie, you're a born nurturer.''

He could picture her with a baby in her arms, suckling at her breast. Whoa…lose that picture. Then it dawned on him that Ana could already have a child.

"You think you have me all figured out, don't you?'' she questioned him. "You're so sure that I have someone waiting for me to come home.'' She looked thoughtful and he knew she was trying to remember something. "I don't feel that way at all.''

"I have to commend you. For someone who survived a crash and doesn't even know her name, you've handled it well.''

"I have no choice.''

"I know it seems you've been here forever, but the rain will stop. A rescue team will come looking for the plane.''

She smiled. "I don't mind staying here. The only thing I've ever minded was…''

"Me,'' Jake finished. "I know I've been difficult. I'll try and do better.''

She nodded and pushed her empty plate away. "So you're going to turn into the perfect cabin mate."

"That's a stretch, but I'll try."

"Oh, my, I don't know if I can stand it. Now, if only the rain would stop, life would be perfect."

"That's one thing I can't do anything about."

She looked indignant. "Then what use are you to me?"

"I'm a pretty good poker player."

"Poker? I not sure I know what that is?"

He grinned. "Wow…could I take advantage of this." He stood and crossed the room to the desk by the fireplace, opened a drawer and took out a deck of cards. "It's a card game. I take it you've never heard of it."

"Can I guess that you're going to teach me?"

"Unless, you want to do something else all day."

She looked down at her hands. "I could stand a manicure and a bath—a nice long bubble bath. But they can wait. Okay, Mr. Sanderstone, ante up."

"Oh, no, I think I'm being had?"

"Only if you want to be," she said and stood to clear the table.

"Hey, stop doing my job." He covered her hand with his and sparks shot through him.

Ana pulled back. "I'll do the dishes and you can bring in some more wood. The cabin is a little cool."

Hell, he was burning up. Ana had that effect on him. And worse, he liked it.

"I have two pairs," Ana said, with a straight face.

Jake cursed under his breath and tossed his cards on the table. "I think you've been lying to me, chère. This isn't the first time you've played this game."

She shrugged innocently. "How would I know? I have no memory."

"You've also won the last three hands. If I didn't know better I'd think you're cheating."

She gasped. "Why, Jake, what a terrible thing to accuse a person of. I'm insulted."

"Yeah, right. Now tell me, how are you doing it?"

Ana didn't know herself, but there was something familiar about this game. "Truly, I've just been lucky," she said as she scooted the wooden matches to her side of the table. "I probably played before, but I don't remember." She brushed her hair from her face. Some strands had come loose from the rubber band that held it. She groaned at the annoyance. "This hair is so annoying and filthy. If it's not too much trouble, may I wash it tonight?"

"No problem. We'll just heat some water."

"I don't know how you stand it without running water."

"It's not a problem for me."

"Not if you don't like to bathe."

"I bathe, in the creek."

The erotic picture of Jake standing naked in the stream sent her pulse racing. "I could stand in the front of cabin and do that, but I'm not crazy about cold showers."

"How about a metal tub with heated water?"

Her mouth gaped open. "You mean, inside here where it's warm and I can use soap and shampoo?"

"I don't have any of that flowery scented soap."

"I don't care, I just want to be able to submerge my body in water." The only washing she'd done in the past week had been out of a small basin.

"Okay, after supper I'll bring in the tub and we'll

heat some water." He raised an eyebrow. "Is this going to get me off breakfast duty tomorrow?"

She smiled back and teased. "If I get a hot bath, you can have anything."

Jake managed to empty the rainwater out of the large metal tub on the porch. Easy job. The thing was heavy, but on its side, he managed to roll it into the cabin. The warmest spot in the room was next to the fire, but by the stove he had heat and it wasn't far from the water.

Pushing aside the table, he placed the barrel there. It wasn't as big as he'd liked, but Ana could fit. He flashed to a picture of her slender naked body...

Jake shook away the wayward thought, then turned to the sink, set a bucket under the spigot and began to pump. Twenty minutes later, he filled half the tub with cold water, while Ana supervised the hot water. All four burners were going and every pot in the place was being used for the job. By the time they dumped the hot in, steam rose from the tub, forming beads of sweat on their faces.

"I think that's enough," Jake said. "We don't want it to overflow."

"It's perfect." Ana looked around the room. "Except, it's a little out in the open and I hate to send you outside."

"Got an idea." He went over by the door and uncoiled a thin rope attached to the wall. "It's a clothesline." He took one end and walked across to the cupboard and wrapped it around the knob. Then from the bedroom, he retrieved a sheet and draped it over the line. "How's that?"

"Oh, Jake. It's perfect."

He opened the cupboard and took out a bar of soap and a towel. "It's not the Ritz, but I think it will work."

She took the items from him. "I guess I better get on with it before the water turns cold."

That was his cue to get lost. "Take all the time you need."

He walked across the small room to the hearth. Needing to keep the place warm, he tossed several more logs on the fire. A rustling sound from behind the sheet drew his curiosity and he turned around. His throat suddenly went dry. The oil lamp on the counter threw enough light for him to see through the sheet. Ana's silhouette taunted him with what he couldn't have. He averted his gaze and stared out the window at the nice cold rain.

"Oh, Jake. This is heaven."

That didn't help. He heard her splash water in the tub. He pictured Ana scooping it up in her hands and letting it run over her body. When she sighed in pleasure, his body sprang to life. He closed his eyes, fighting the desire he'd been so expert at controlling. For years he'd honed the ability to reveal nothing, especially his feelings. It was his preservation, his survival. With Ana around, he was losing the battle.

It was the simplest of comforts, but Ana would never take a bath for granted again. She wet her hair first, poured a small amount of shampoo in her hand then massaged it into her hair. After rinsing from the pail on the floor, she wrung out the excess water, then leaned back to enjoy her bath.

"Have I told you what a nice man you are, Jake Sanderstone?"

"Having a good time?" She could hear the smile in his voice.

"Oh, my, yes. Who would have thought a simple bath could feel this wonderful." She slid down as far as she could go in the metal vessel, then rested her head against the cabinet door. Raising one leg, she wished for a razor. She started to voice her request, then thought better of it. Jake had done enough. Besides kissing her senseless, the man could cook, and now, given her her heart's desire. If only he would give in to his own desires.

Last night he had…for a while. A shiver went down her spine. He'd wanted more than a kiss, and so had she. She closed her eyes and recalled his touch, his lips coaxing hers to open for him. Remembering the feel of his body pressed against hers, she stifled a moan. There couldn't be another man in her life. Not when she wanted Jake so badly. Although stubborn, she'd come to care for him. And if he wasn't so noble, he would admit he wanted her, too. Their time together would end soon, and she'd never see him again. Sadness overcame her, and she realized she was thinking about leaving the man she'd come to love.

Jake gritted his teeth. Before he went crazy, he had to get Ana out of the bath, and dressed. "Hey, you about finished?"

"I should be," she said grudgingly. "I'm about to turn into a prune. Not very attractive."

"A person could only hope," he muttered.

"Did you say something?"

"No," he answered.

Hearing the water slosh, Jake looked up just as Ana rose from the tub. His heart tripped as he watched her lift her long arms over her head to brush back her hair. She turned sideways, showing off her full breasts and his body went rigid. Every movement she made only added to the fire simmering in him.

She reached for a towel and wrapped it around her body. Slowly, deliberately, she drew the sheet back and stepped out clad only in a towel. All hope of figuring out this woman fled.

"Ana..." he said, but he couldn't form another word.

She gave him a shy smile. "I can't tell you how wonderful I feel," she said, then boldly walked across the room finally stopping in front of him. She reached out and touched his face, then her hands moved down to his chest and even through his shirt, her heat burned his skin.

"Maybe...it would be a good idea if you get dressed."

She shook her head. "Bad idea, Jake. And if you're honest with yourself, you'll admit you don't want me to be dressed, either."

"What I want isn't relevant here." His voice sounded strange even to him. "It's the best and the safest way to stay out of trouble. And to avoid any regrets."

Ana's hands were shaking. This feeling, the unbearable ache was something she wouldn't forget. "I don't want safe, Jake. And I won't have any regrets..."

When he tried to disagree, she placed a finger over his lips. "I want to feel," she went on. "To feel like I did last night. I want to be in your arms, I want you to hold me." She closed her eyes. "I don't want to be alone anymore. Jake...I need—"

His resistance melted and he pulled her into his arms. Holding her close, he nuzzled the side of her neck. "God, woman, you're too damn tempting for your own good."

"Thank you. You're tempting, too." She raised her arms to circle his neck, her towel dropping dangerously low.

His hands caressed her back, sending new and wondrous sensations through her. Not to mention what his thighs did every time they brushed against her bare legs.

He raised his head and looked at her with those deep-set dark eyes. "You know we're both in over our heads. But you have me so crazy I can't think anymore. I want you, Ana." When his mouth closed over hers in a searing kiss, her legs gave out, but he caught her and held her tight.

His tongue touched her lips, seeking entry. When she yielded, his breath caught and his hold tightened. Immediately the kiss changed and heated as he teased and coaxed her. He wrenched his mouth away to trail a line of kisses down her jaw to the top of her breasts.

Ana moaned softly as his day-old beard scraped against her sensitized skin. She wanted more. One by one, she managed to undo the buttons of his shirt until his chest was gloriously bare, except for a swirl of dark hair. Bravely, she ran her fingertips over his skin, feeling him shudder, reveling in the fact she had caused it. She watched his face as she pushed his shirt off, then took the time to admire the breadth of his shoulders and the power of his arms. His eyes blazed down at her and she could feel his control slipping away.

With a growl, he captured her mouth in another

heated kiss, then scooped her up in his arms and carried her to the couch. He laid her down and feasted on her mouth as his hand tugged at the towel.

"I want you, Ana," he breathed. "From the moment I saw you I wanted you like this."

She swallowed hard. "I want you too, Jake."

The towel came free and her breasts were exposed to him. "Beautiful," he whispered, trying to hold on to the last of his control. He reached out and cupped her in his hand, then he bent his head and took the nipple into his mouth. Her quickened breath urged him on as he paid homage to the other one, circling the puckered bud with his tongue.

"Jake," she cried. Her fingers combed through his hair, holding him against her.

The sweet urgency in her voice nearly drove Jake over the edge. No other woman had gotten to him this way. No other woman had made him so reckless, he couldn't think about anything except how desperately he wanted her. He stretched out beside her on the couch, fitting her perfectly against his body, enjoying the wild sensation of her breasts rubbing along his chest. A sense of rightness settled over him. For a short time he would live the fantasy, believing that she would be his.

"Oh, please," Ana begged, unable to get close enough to ease the ache. Something inside her coiled tighter and tighter. Her lips met Jake's and she tried to relay her hunger. What she wanted. Him. She raised her body, feeling his heat, but needing more. She closed her eyes, as his hands moved over her, making her tingle, making her crazy.

Then it happened. A picture flashed behind her eyelids. A face. It flashed again. A child—no children.

There were three of them. They were all happy and laughing.

She gasped and sat up.

"Ana, what's wrong?" Jake asked as he rolled away, giving her room.

She closed her eyes again, but the scene was gone. "I saw something."

"What?"

Shaking her head, she gripped the towel and covered herself. "I'm not sure. I saw a child's face, then another. There were three of them. But I didn't recognize any of them." Ana felt the tears coming, but she couldn't let them fall.

As much as she tried to hang on to him, Ana could feel Jake withdraw. Standing, he went to the other side of the room. He picked up his shirt on the way.

"Jake..." She needed him so desperately, but she couldn't help but feel guilty. Were the children hers?

He raised a hand. "I don't think anything you say right now will help this situation." He paced around, looking edgy, as if he wanted to hit something.

"Jake, please talk to me."

"What do you want me to say?" He stared at her, unbelieving. "Okay, then I'll say it. Those were your children you saw. And we just nearly made a huge mistake."

Chapter Seven

"How soon before the search planes can go back out?" Colonel Prescott asked the captain.

"Sometime within the next forty-eight hours. The weather bureau says the storm will be moving out of the area by then."

"Bloody hell, she would be dead by then," Pierce said. "If the princess survived the damn crash to begin with, she is up there in weather conditions that could kill the best trained SEALs. There has to be some way to get in. What about the locals?"

"Sir, they've been combing the terrain on foot, but the area is pretty treacherous. They were making headway until the storm moved in again. The good news is we're getting a weak signal from the plane's ELT." The captain went to the map on the wall and pointed to a region in the upper range of the Cambrian Mountains. "So we're concentrating our efforts here."

"That not good enough, Captain."

Both men turned around to discover that Queen Marissa had come into the room. Pierce along with the Captain bowed from the waist.

"Your Majesty," he said, then walked across the room to greet her. She offered her hand and he escorted her to the chair in front of his desk.

Queen Marissa was strikingly beautiful with her dark hair and blue eyes. Dressed in a taupe-colored business suit, she graced a briefing room as well as she did a ballroom. Born to privilege, she carried the title of queen with grace and ease. Even during the trials of late, she'd been composed and carried on her duties without complaint. She was also mother to his sweet Meredith.

"How is the search going?"

Pierce dismissed the captain and closed the door. He motioned to the other chair and waited for the queen's nodded permission to join her.

"Please, have a seat." She folded her hands together in her lap. "Just tell me how you plan to bring my daughter home."

"Your Majesty, we are doing everything humanly possible to find Anastasia. But I feel I should prepare you for the possibility…"

The queen shook her head. "No, Pierce, she is alive. I would know if something had happened to my child. In my heart, I know she's out there. We just have to find her before danger reaches her."

Before he could answer, the desk phone rang. He excused himself and picked it up.

"Prescott, here," he announced.

"Pierce, it's Cole. I was told Queen Marissa was with you. May I speak with her?"

Certainly." He held out the receiver to the Queen,

knowing she awaited news about the investigation of the American twins, possible heirs to the throne. "It's Cole Everson from Chicago."

She nodded and leaned back in the chair. "Please, put him on the speakerphone."

He pressed the button and hung up the receiver. "Go ahead."

"Your Majesty," Cole said.

"Yes, Mr. Everson. What do you have to report?"

"I'm afraid it's not the news we hoped for," Cole said.

"As head of the Royal Intelligence, Mr. Everson, I would think you could do this job. If not, I'm sure I can find someone else…"

"No, Your Majesty, I have located one of the American twins, Marcus Cordello. I just haven't been able to get to meet with me."

Pierce's jaw clenched. He would like nothing better than to get his hands on Broderick Penwyck. Pierce didn't care if he was the king's brother, the bastard, had wreaked havoc on this country for far too long. Years ago, Broderick had masterminded a plot to switch the twins at birth to be raised by a rich American family. He then arranged for the King's newborns to be replaced with two other fraternal twin boys. The queen discovered the plan and stopped it, but she never told the King. But she would like to find the suspected heirs in America. She had located Marcus Cordello.

"As I said," the queen spoke, "if you can't do your job, I will find someone else who will." Marissa stood. "Gentlemen, I expect to hear from you soon." She turned and walked out of the room, leaving no doubt she would do just that.

* * *

Ana knew in her heart she had never loved any man before Jake.

For the past hour, she hadn't moved from the couch, except to put on a shirt. Staring into the dying fire, she'd been trying everything she could think of to stir up more memories. Nothing worked. Just bits and pieces of a puzzle that might never be completed. Could she accept that? Could she go back to a life that she didn't remember? Love a family she no longer knew? What about a man? She knew her feelings for Jake were strong. In her heart she knew she didn't have a so-called lover. She would know it. No man had touched her the way Jake had. No man's kisses had made her forget to breathe.

The cabin door opened and Jake came in along with a chilling wind. He didn't look any happier than he had when he left her. His eyes told of his misery. She wanted to go to him. Comfort him. She, too, needed reassurance, needed to know that he had felt something for her, that she wasn't alone.

Jake went to the hearth, removed the screen and added more wood. "Lord, woman, you would freeze to death if I wasn't around." He finally looked at her, his dark eyes showed his torment.

"Jake," she began, hoping he would look at her. He did. "I didn't want to…to stop. The memory just startled me."

He glanced away, as if the contact was too painful. "We didn't have a choice, Ana. I never should have let it go so far."

"But you wouldn't have stopped, if I hadn't had the…vision?"

Jake ground his back teeth together to keep in control. "What do you want me to say, chère? That I wanted you? Yeah, I want you, all right. But don't kid yourself, I have been up here a long time... alone...without a woman. I'm as human as the next guy. You offered yourself to me—"

"No! You care about me, enough to stop things when you thought I could be married," she said, her chin raised.

"I'm not the man you think I am."

"Oh, you're such a bad fellow."

"And you better remember that, because the next time you play with fire you might just get burned."

She raised her chin defiantly, but couldn't hide a slight quiver in her lips. "Oh, I'll remember." Her voice grew soft and seductive. "I'll remember the man with the gentle touch and the kisses that took my breath away...."

He closed his eyes to shut out her words. "Stop it! In the heat of passion, a man will do about anything to get what he wants. So don't make the mistake of trusting me. Believe me, you'll regret it." As if struck by a bullet, pain shot through him. Then he felt Ana's hand against his arm. He fought to pull away, but he couldn't.

"I will never regret anything between you and I, Jake."

Push her away, he told himself. "Just give it time and you will."

"I don't need time," she assured him. "I trust you with my life."

He had to move away, she was tempting him again. "So did Meg and it cost her."

Jealousy surged through Ana. Did he love another woman? "Who's Meg?"

He cocked an eyebrow. "You're full of questions."

"You seem to think I have a man in my life, is it so strange for me to wonder about the woman in yours?" She hated the possessiveness she felt, but she couldn't push it aside. "What was she like?"

He shrugged. "I'm not sure I can tell you. Not because I don't want to, but because I never took the time to really know Meg. She was my partner."

"She worked for the FBI?"

He nodded. "We were assigned to an undercover task force in Montana to watch a militia group. We posed as a married couple wanting to join their cause. I guess we played the part pretty well."

It was one question she didn't want to ask, but she had to know. "Did you love her?"

He didn't seem surprised by the question. "We both had too much baggage from our pasts to believe in true love. We got along. The sex was good."

Ana couldn't stop the heat rushing to her face. "I wish I could remember if sex was good," she murmured.

He tensed. "You can stop looking at me like that, because I'm not going to help jar your memory."

She rested her chin on her hands. "Jake, we both wanted what happened between us. So how can you regret it."

He released a long breath. "You're not making this easy on me, are you?"

"I just want you to know how I feel. I don't expect anything from you."

"Good, because until we know who you are, we can't let anything happen."

She wanted to jump for joy. "That means if I discover who I am...you mean...we can be together?"

"No!" He drew a breath and released it slowly. "That means I return to the crash site to try and find out who you are."

"You're not going without me."

"Right, I'm not, you're coming with me. Maybe seeing the wreckage will trigger something."

Her eyes lit up, then died as quickly. "What if it doesn't?"

"Then we'll handle it. Besides, someone has to be looking for you."

She never felt more alone. "Then why haven't they?"

"This weather is holding off any search. They might know where the plane went down by the tracking system, but in this rugged terrain they'll have to wait. With any luck tomorrow we'll get some answers."

She felt better. It had been ten days. Not that she hated being with Jake, but she wanted desperately to know her identity. "Thanks for allowing me to come along."

"As if you'd let me go alone." He forced a smile. "I'll go check on the horses, and you better get to bed. If the weather is improved we'll hike to the site tomorrow." He turned toward the door.

Ana had one more question. "Jake."

He paused but didn't turn around. "What?"

She suddenly felt shy, but needed to know. "What happened with Meg? Do you...and she...? Were you going to marry her?"

He had a faraway look in his eyes, then said, "Yeah. Then she died...and I couldn't do a damn thing to stop it."

The rain was light, and even in her too-large boots and long underwear under a pair of Jake's jeans, Ana managed to keep up. Max was leading them as Jake and Ana made the hike over the ridge and into the ravine.

Ana drew a long breath. "I can't believe you carried me all the way back to the cabin," she said. Her voice slowly died as she looked over the destruction. "Oh, God…this is horrible." Then suddenly sounds exploded in her head. A screeching of metal and her own screams. Her heart began to race, making her feel light-headed.

"Ana, what's wrong?"

She shook her head. "I just heard this awful sound in my head. I think I was reliving the crash."

"Do you remember anything else?"

"No."

"Then come on, let's get started," he said. "The weather might not hold."

Jake took her hand and escorted her through the broken trees until they passed the tail of the jet, then came upon the midsection.

"I can't believe it held together."

"Thank God it did," he told her.

They went inside, the roof keeping the rain off. Ana pushed back her hood and wiped the moisture from her face. She glanced around the battered compartment, the bent and torn metal, hoping to find something familiar.

"From what I could tell, you were sitting here." He showed her the dark stain on the upholstery. "That's your blood on the seat. When Max and I arrived, you weren't here. Max tracked you over to a group of trees. You somehow got out when the fire started. It ended quickly, thanks to the heavy rain.''

Ana could still smell the smoke as she searched through the rubble that had been thrown around. She hoped to come across a purse, anything that could tell her who she was. Where she came from.

Jake was on his knees, searching under the seats, going through the compartments. Then when it seemed hopeless, he located a metal box from under the same chair Ana had sat during the flight.

"Look what I found," Jake said as he held up the box.

"What is it?"

"Could be anything, from a first-aid kit to a tool-box.''

Using a screwdriver he'd found, Jake popped it open. He took out a canvas pouch that had Penwyck Mining stamped across the front.

"Well, it's from Penwyck." Jake opened it and shook out the contents. Several large milky-white crystals fell out.

"Oh, my," Ana gasped. "What are those stones?"

Jake picked one up, weighed the pyramid-shaped stones in his hand, then held it up to the light. The stone was about seven carats and one of the smallest of the dozen in the bag. "I'm not an expert, but my guess is diamonds."

"Diamonds. Why were they under my seat?"

"That's the sixty-four-thousand-dollar question, chère—or should I say the two-million-dollar question?" He had his own thoughts. "Somebody was smuggling the diamonds from Penwyck."

"Who would do that?" Ana looked at Jake, her eyes wide and innocent, then her anger flared. "You think I'm somehow involved in taking the diamonds, don't you?''

''I didn't say that,'' he argued. He didn't want to believe it. There had to be another explanation. ''Look, the day I buried the two bodies, I discovered the pilot was a member of the Black Knights.''

She looked puzzled. Either she was one hell of an actress, or she didn't have a clue what was going on. Jake suspected the latter.

''I told you when you came back from burying Rory, I don't know anything about the Black Knights.''

''They're a subversive group,'' he told her.

''And one was the pilot?''

He nodded. ''Yes. We have to figure out what he was doing with Rory Hearne a Penwyck security guard.''

''Wonderful. Everyone seems to know who they are except me. There's got to be something around here that will tell me who I am.'' Ana pulled up her rain hood and stepped outside.

This was worse than she could ever imagine. What if she was connected to these Black Knights and the stolen diamonds? No, she refused to believe that, and somehow, she was going to prove it.

First she went to the pine tree and found two rocky mounds. Jake had done a nice job on the graves. It caused Ana to think about how vulnerable she was. Two people had already died in the crash. Two men who could have been smuggling diamonds. How did she fit into it all?

Fighting frustration she began her search, for anything, a purse or a notebook. Anything that would tell her who she was. She found papers from the cockpit and called Jake over, showing him that they'd taken off from Penwyck Airport early the morning of the crash. She found soaked pillows and blankets as she kept digging through the rubble until she came upon a smaller notebook.

She wiped off the burgundy leather cover, exposing three engraved initials A.E.P. A strange feeling went through her. She recognized it. Fear froze her and she couldn't open it.

"Jake," she called and rushed over to him.

"What is it?"

"I found this." She handed the notebook to him.

Jake studied the leather cover and lingered on the initials. This didn't belong to Loden or Hearne. This book was going to tell him something. Was he ready? Unable to delay the inevitable, he opened it and found a calendar. The month of September was showing with several dates filled in. They weren't run-of-the-mill business appointments, either.

"Looks like this A.E.P. person is busy. An engagement to attend Penwyck Hospital's charity dinner."

Jake went through the rest of the book, noting several different society functions were included, many had been held at the palace with the king and queen. He glanced at Ana and saw the charm around her neck. He had no doubt who she was. He just couldn't rejoice in it. It suddenly felt as if the air had been robbed from his lungs as raw emotions raced through him, ripping at his gut. He wanted to close his eyes and wish it away, something he'd tried as a kid. It hadn't worked then and it wasn't going to work now.

Somehow he managed to walk to the midsection of the jet, Ana close on his heels. The outside of the plane had been burned in the fire, some of the paint had peeled off, but some of the lettering remained. He vigorously rubbed off the soot the rain hadn't washed away. Underneath, he found the faint outline of a crest and the name Penwyck across the bottom. The last of the proof. That explained why a Penwyck security person had been on the plane. Rory Hearne was more than likely a bodyguard. Ana's bodyguard.

"Jake, what did you discover?"

He looked at Ana, seeing her in a new light. Although the rain had plastered down her hair, and her face was scrubbed clean of any makeup, she carried herself with poise and beauty. He should have known she was a princess the way she acted always expecting to have things done for her—expecting the attention she deserved.

Ana stamped her foot. "Will you tell me?"

His defenses rose. "Don't tell me you're still having trouble remembering, Ana. Or should I say, Princess Anastasia?" He bowed.

Her eyes widened. "Are you sure?"

He pointed to the crest on the plane's side. "Rory was probably your bodyguard. What I don't know is how a member of the Black Knights came to be your pilot. Maybe Hearne was in on it, too." He shook his head. "It's hard to believe, with the reputation of your country's Royal Elite Team, they let diamonds be smuggled out of the country."

"Stop talking so fast, I don't know any of this…." Ana stopped and a strange look came over her face. "No, I do remember Rory," she said as if she didn't believe it herself. "I remember him. He was going with me to London. We left early to avoid the storm, but we ran into it anyway. The entire plane was bouncing around. I heard the pilot radio for help. Then we started to go down and Rory called back from the cockpit and told me to put the cushions around me." She wiped the tears off her face.

Jake grabbed her, suddenly jealous that she'd shed tears for another man. "What do you remember, Ana? Was Hearne your lover?"

She jerked away and shook her head. "No! He was my friend. And I know that Rory wouldn't have anything to do with smuggling diamonds."

"How can you be so sure?"

"In my heart, I know it. I didn't know the pilot. I don't think I even saw his face. At least I don't remember it." Her eyes pleaded with him. "You believe that I didn't have anything to do with this. Don't you?"

He nodded. "You have no reason to steal. Your family is royalty." The words came out sounding caustic. But to him, Ana being a princess was almost worse than her being involved with someone.

"How do you know that?"

"Your family owns an entire island. In fact, they've been in the news a lot lately. Your brother was kidnapped recently. In fact, it was the Black Knights who claimed responsibility."

She gasped. "My brother?"

He nodded. "He was returned back home safely."

"So that's where I'll be going, too. Whenever I get rescued."

"No, Princess," he said as he pulled the bag of diamonds from his pocket. "Now the stakes are a lot higher. The good guys and the bad guys are both going to be looking for you." He held up his hand. "And these gems."

Chapter Eight

She was a *princess!*

Jake still couldn't believe it as they trekked back to the cabin. Of all the people to crash-land on his mountain, he had to get a princess. He wiped the rain from his face. Hell, if he'd had any crazy ideas about starting something up with Ana, they were scratched now.

She was hands off. He thought back to last night, remembering how close he'd come to giving in to the temptation. She'd had him so tied up in knots that he couldn't think. Her innocent seduction nearly turned into a disaster. He climbed over the rocky terrain and glanced back at Ana as she easily maneuvered the slick trail. She looked ridiculous in the too-big raincoat and boots. Her wet hair was plastered against her face. Her beautiful face. He hadn't been able to get last night out his mind. It was sinful how much he wanted her. How close he'd come to making love to her.

She had him thinking about things he'd never thought about before. Commitment. Marriage.

What a laugh. The princess and the ex-government agent. What had he been thinking? Truth was, he hadn't been thinking at all. Not since he'd found her.

Well, he was thinking today.

It was his job to keep her safe until someone came for her. But who would that someone be? Penwyck's military or the Black Knights? If the Knights managed to locate the crash site and didn't find the diamonds, they were going to come looking for them. He touched the bag of gems in his pocket. Having dealt with subversives before, he knew that they didn't play by the rules, and innocent lives were expendable when it came to their cause. So he knew nothing was going to stop them. Once the road cleared and was safe, they would be coming.

Jake hoped the Penwyck government would have a better bead on where the plane had gone down, because he didn't have much in the way of weapons to hold off these guys—just the 9mm Glock that he confiscated from Rory, and an old hunting rifle back at the cabin were it. The element of surprise would be his best defense to protect Ana. And he would give his life to save hers.

"How soon before we're back at the cabin?"

"Not long. What's the matter, Princess, you getting tired?"

Ana glared at him. "No, what I am getting weary of is your sullen attitude. Suddenly there is something wrong with me because of who my parents are."

Jake couldn't help but laugh. "They rule a country."

"Is that my fault? Is that a reason to reject me?"

She pushed past him. "Take me home, Max." The animal looked at Jake, then with a bark, took off along the trail.

She even had his dog following her commands. Ana raised that stubborn chin and something tightened around his heart. Then she turned and marched off.

Jake knew then he was the one in danger.

Back at the cabin, Ana changed into fresh clothes, then went to sit by the fire to warm up and dry her hair. Ever since Jake had discovered her identity, he'd been ignoring her. Why would he be so upset? She was the one who just learned who she was, not him. What was even more distressing, she still had no awareness of her family.

Anastasia Penwyck was just a name to her. She still had no memory. Except for remembering that she had sisters, everything else was blank. Not even a flash of their faces. A sudden longing gripped her as she thought about her parents. Why couldn't she remember them? She had a family, but there were still no images of her father, or her mother. Were they alive?

"Jake, are my parents living?"

He nodded, then returned to his job of stoking the fire. "The media showed pictures of both of them when your brother Owen was returned safely to Penwyck."

Jake, too, had changed clothes. He'd put on a red and black plaid flannel shirt and jeans so worn she could see white along the thighs and across his rear. In fact, there was a small tear starting at the base of the pocket.

He turned around and caught her watching him.

Her face heated up. "Did you see any other members of my family? Maybe I was in the picture." Suddenly she was hungry for any news.

"Stop trying so hard," he told her. "I have a feeling that when you see your family, your memory will return."

"We still have to get off this mountain."

"And we will."

"Before the Black Knights show up?" she asked. Tears filled her eyes and she rose from the hearth and went to the window.

He followed her. "I'm not going to let anything happen to you, chère." As soon as the too-familiar nickname came out, he stiffened. "I'm sorry, I shouldn't have called you that."

"Why is it any different now? I'm the same person as before you found out about my family."

"No, you are not. You're a princess."

"No, I'm the woman you wanted to make love to," she argued. "I think you still want me."

He puffed out a breath. "Stop pushing this, Ana. You and I both know whatever nearly happened last night was a mistake."

"Why? We wanted each other."

Jake raked his fingers through his hair. "You are the most infuriating woman. Wanting doesn't make it right."

"It makes it very right. I'm not married."

"You could belong to someone. He wouldn't want his future bride to be with another man."

"How many times do I have to tell you there isn't anyone else?" she insisted. "Besides, I wouldn't agree to marrying someone I didn't love." Ana placed her hands on his chest. She loved the fact that heart was pounding beneath her fingertips. "But you…"

She raised up on her toes and placed a kiss against his mouth. When he didn't move, she wondered if he could resist her, then he pulled her closer as his mouth captured hers. He took little time for finesse as he parted her lips, then pushed his tongue inside her mouth, revealing his need for her. Ana pressed her body against his and reveled in the fact that he wanted her as much as she wanted him.

He finally broke off the kiss. "This isn't right," he said.

She refused to listen. "Oh, yes, this is very right."

He stepped back. "Ana, we can't do this. We don't belong together. You'll be going back to your family soon. I'm staying here."

"I can stay here, too." She said the words, even though she realized it would never happen.

He laughed. "Chere, you are crazy if you think your father, the *king,* will allow you to stay with a unemployed FBI agent. I don't have any job prospects, not to mention, the difference in our ages."

"There can't be that much difference."

"Nearly ten years. But with the life I've lived, it might as well be many more." Ana had been protected from the world; he'd seen the evil firsthand.

"What does any of that matter if we care about each other?"

"To me it matters. A lot. I came here because of things that happened…in my job. You don't really know me. I'm not the man you think I am."

"Yes, you are."

He shook his head. "I've had to do things to survive…" His words drifted off. He couldn't tell her, even if it would drive her away. "You said so yourself. Look, I'm moody and hard to get along with."

"And you're also funny and caring. And if you'd let yourself, you would care about me."

She wasn't listening to a word he'd said. "It can't last, Ana. You have responsibilities to your family. I wouldn't fit into your life there. I don't fit in a lot of places," he went on. "As for family, I didn't even know who my father was. My mother drank too much. I'm a street kid. I learned to survive the hard way. I did things that I'm not proud of."

Ana heard a sadness in his voice that nearly broke her heart. She wanted to cry for the boy who'd had no one to turn to. "I'm sorry, Jake. No child should have to grow up that way."

"I don't want your damn pity," he spat at her. "I survived because I wanted out and I got out. I did it on my own, without anyone's help. I liked it that way."

"It isn't pity, Jake. You're the man you are today because of your determination, because you wanted a better life. I could cry for the boy who had to go through such a horrendous childhood." She wanted desperately to reach out to him. "But you're mistaken about one thing, Jake. No one wants to be alone."

"Well, I will be, just as soon as the road is fit to travel." His face was stone cold. "I'm taking you down the mountain and turning you over to the authorities…along with the diamonds."

She tried to hide her hurt. "I'm sure my father will gladly compensate you for all your trouble."

"I don't want a damn thing."

"But you found the diamonds."

"And I'm giving them back."

He pulled the bag from his jacket pocket and tossed it on the table. "They're yours."

She didn't want them, either. "I wish we'd never found them."

"That doesn't change who you are, or the fact that there are people who want those diamonds."

"And they would come up here, no matter what?" She shivered involuntarily.

Jake didn't want to talk about the possible danger Ana could be in. "I'm not going to let anything happen to you. Besides, it isn't easy to get in or out of here. The nearest town is seven miles away, and the only road to this cabin washed out with the same storm that brought down your plane. Until the rain stops and it dries out, even a four-wheel drive vehicle couldn't make it up the road."

"These men might," she said. "We were able to get to the crash site."

"We're already on the mountain. It'll be difficult to get here, especially with these weather conditions."

Her eyes grew wide. "If the Black Knights make it here, shouldn't we be prepared?"

"I will be." Jake planned on standing guard at night. He grabbed the bag of diamonds off the table. "I'm not giving these away easily, but I may have to use them to barter with."

Jake went into the bedroom. He pushed the bed aside, found the loose floorboard and popped out the strip of wood. After stuffing the canvas bag into the hole, he replaced the board. Slipping the bed back in its position, he turned around and found Ana standing at the door. Did she think he was going keep them?

"Don't worry, I'm not going to run off with the goods if that's what you think." He hated the harsh words the second he'd said them. Didn't she realize he was only trying to protect her?

"I know what you're trying to do, Jake."

"Good. Why don't you fill me in?" he asked.

"I can take care of myself, you know. You're not responsible for my safety."

"Anything else I need to know."

She stared at him. "Plenty, but I'm not sure if you're ready to hear it yet."

"I'm sure you'll tell me when the time is right."

Ana gave him the once-over, letting her gaze move slowly, lingering on his magnificent body. She was glad to see his breathing begin to change. So the man wasn't as immune as he pretended to be.

When she raised her gaze to his, she felt her own breathing begin to quicken. His eyes were so mesmerizing, she just wanted to lose herself in their dark depths.

She walked to him. "Oh, I will. I'll tell you exactly what I want to do with you...then maybe I'll make some suggestions on what you can do with me."

A thrill rushed through her when Jake's jaw twitched and his hands fisted. She wanted to go into his arms, but she knew he'd only reject her. He wasn't ready to listen to anything she had to say. She still hadn't remembered much about her life. There were stolen diamonds to think about and one other major thing to consider.

She just happened to be a princess. Funny, even that couldn't help her get the man she loved.

Just as darkness fell that night, Jake walked from the shed back to the cabin. He'd checked to make sure everything was secured outside. Earlier, he'd taken the handgun out of the drawer and loaded it. After so many years with the bureau, he'd felt naked without one. Thanks to Herane, he wasn't going to be unprepared for any unwelcome visitors.

He stepped onto the porch where Max lay by the door. "What's the matter, guy, get kicked out?" He got a whine from the animal as he rubbed behind the dog's ears. "Come on, let's go inside and see what we can come up with for dinner."

Jake opened the door to find that Ana had been busy during the time he'd been gone. The table had been moved closer to the fireplace, was set for dinner and he smelled food.

In the kitchen area he found Ana at the stove. Surprisingly, she was busy stirring what he thought would be dinner in a pot. That wasn't what bothered him. It was the way she was dressed. Gone were the jeans she'd had on earlier, she was only wearing one of his shirts and a pair of socks. He glanced over at the fireplace and again, he saw her freshly washed underwear drying on the hearth.

Oh Lord, she was naked underneath. He had no doubt she had plans for the evening. Well, he was going to nix them right now.

Ana looked at him and smiled. "Dinner is ready," she announced. "I prepared some stew." She carried the pot to the table and dished out some in each bowl. She went back to the kitchen, retrieved a hot pad, then opened the oven door and pulled out what looked like biscuits.

She glanced over her shoulder. "Jake, would you please wash up?"

"Oh, sure." As he walked to the sink, he looked down at the half-full tub and memories of last night stirred his desires again. He quickly pushed the scene out of his head and began to pump the water. After wiping off his hands, he sat down.

Smiling, Ana unfolded a napkin and placed it on her lap. "I suspect my parents spent a lot of money to teach me etiquette. They should be happy to know that even amnesia couldn't rid me of my manners."

Jake couldn't help but admire her natural grace. It made him feel so clumsy around her. He picked up a warm biscuit. "I thought you didn't cook."

"I assume somewhere in my education, I learned. Besides, all I had to do was read your cookbook. It took me a couple of tries, but I was determined to show you how I can compromise."

"I'd say you've compromised a lot just having to stay here."

She raised an eyebrow. "Have I complained?"

He took a bite of food and shook his head.

"And I'm grateful for everything you've done for me," she said. "I'll never be able to thank you enough."

"No need," he said. The last thing he wanted was her gratitude. What he wanted, he couldn't have.

"Well, I've decided to start paying you back. I'll do the cooking. And as a bigger treat I'm going to heat some water so tonight you can bathe."

The biscuit got stuck in Jake's throat. He reached for his glass of water and took several swallows. The food finally went down. "That's not necessary."

"Oh, yes it is. And since the tub is already inside and half-filled, all I have to do is heat up some water. Don't look so stern, you'll enjoy it. I enjoyed every bit of last night."

Jake knew she was up to something, but he wasn't about to fall in with her plan. "I don't need a bath."

She wrinkled her nose. "I say you do. What are you afraid of Jake?" She raised her eyebrows. "Afraid I might get a peak at your bum?"

"That's the least of my worries."

"Something must be bothering you." She took a spoonful of food.

"A lot of things are bothering me, but taking a bath isn't one of them."

"That's good. Then you can relax and enjoy it."

He closed his eyes and counted to ten. Infiltrating the Montana militia hadn't caused him as much grief as one stubborn, beautiful princess. He had a feeling the grief was just beginning.

"How are you doing?"

Ana stared at the sheet hanging on the line, surprised she was able to see Jake's silhouette as he sat in the tub.

"This tub isn't one size fits all," he said, then released a sigh. She knew he was beginning to relax.

"But it's not so bad, is it? How long has it been since you've taken a bath in warm water?"

"Too long," he answered his voice low and lazy sounding. "This summer it wasn't too bad washing in the stream, but since it's turned cold…it has been rough. I guess you were right." She could hear the sound of water splashing over him. "This is pretty nice."

A warmth surged through Ana too, as she envisioned an unclothed Jake not twenty feet away. She groaned and sank down on the couch, gazing toward the fire. No, leave him alone, she told herself. Let him bathe in peace. She'd given up on trying to convince the man that they belonged together. He was more stubborn than she was.

Stubbornness was a trait she'd inherited from her father. A sudden shock surged through Ana. Her father. She remembered him, or did she? She couldn't see his face, or hear his voice, but remembered that she and her father had spent time together. She smiled at this new development when she heard Jake's loud curse.

"Damn soap," he spat.

Ana took off across the room and pulled the sheet aside to find Jake sitting in the too small tub, his legs and arms draped over the sides. His long hair was covered in bubbles and he was rubbing his eyes. She bit down on her lip to keep from laughing.

"What the hell do you want?" he asked, seemingly not bothered by her intrusion. He didn't even try to cover himself.

She tried to keep her gaze riveted on his angry face. "It sounded like you needed help." Before he could rebuff her, she went to the sink and poured water in the pail, then added some hot water to the mix.

"I'm capable of washing my hair myself."

"Yes, I'm sure you are. But would it be so bad if you had some help?" She dumped some of the water over his head. He came up sputtering. For a second she thought he was going to climb out of the tub.

"Lady, you are a menace."

"I was only trying to rinse the soap out of your eyes." She handed him a towel, knelt behind him, poured a little shampoo in her hand, then worked it into his thick hair. His grumbles and complaints stopped immediately.

"Now doesn't this feel good?"

He leaned his head back, giving her better access, and said, "Oh, man...don't stop."

"I won't, even if my fingers begin to look like prunes," she promised. She liked having her hands on this man. A deep yearning started low in her stomach, creating a warming sensation. When Jake leaned back further, she could see down the width of his chest; the suds covered anything below the water.

"You're peeking," he said.

She jumped. "I am not. But there isn't much of you that's covered."

He opened one eye. "Want me to stand up and end your curiosity."

"Who says I'm curious?"

He gave her a wicked smile. "The look on your face gives you away."

She hated that he knew her so well. "I don't need to see anything of yours…. I've seen men *starkers* before," she lied.

"I just bet you have."

"Well, you'd lose." She rose, picked up the bucket and poured more water over his head.

He gasped and wiped the water from his face. "What are you trying to do, drown me?"

"It might not be a bad idea."

He stared at her, his dark eyes dilated with desire. Ana glanced down to see that her own shirt was wet and nearly transparent. She couldn't seem to breathe any longer as heat spread through her.

"Maybe you should have tossed *cold* water on me. My thoughts right now are downright sizzlin'." He reached for her and pulled her down to her knees beside the tub, cupping the back of her head and drawing her close.

"Okay, Princess, you got me all hot and bothered. Satisfied?"

His mouth closed over hers in a hungry kiss and Ana reveled in it. She loved the fact he couldn't deny her. She wrapped her arms around his shoulders and pressed herself against him, but the tub prevented true intimacy.

"This is wrong, Ana. So wrong," he groaned.

"It's not. Please…touch me," she whispered and closed her eyes.

Too soon, his mouth worked its way down her jaw to her neck. He unbuttoned her shirt and she boldly guided his head to her breasts.

"Oh, Jake," she cried out as he drew her nipple into his mouth and sucked gently.

He raised his gaze. "You like that?"

"Oh, yes," she sighed.

He gave attention to the other breast, causing her to shiver with need. "Please…don't stop."

He continued his assault as he came back to her mouth. "You taste so damn good, chère. You cause a craving deep inside me."

His words made her daring. "Then why deny yourself." She leaned forward and offered him her mouth.

He gave her a brazen grin and pulled her against him and began slowly rotating his chest against her breasts, causing a sweet abrasion, and sending tingles through her. Making her want…making her need more.

"Jake, please…"

"Please what?" he asked, taking teasing bites along her lower lips. "You want more of this?" His lips closed over hers in a heated kiss, then all too soon he released her. "Or this?" His mouth lowered to her breast and sucked the sensitive bud until she cried out.

Suddenly he pulled away. That was when Ana finally heard Max whining and scratching at the cabin door.

Gripping the counter, Jake pulled himself out of the tub as water splashed over the sides and onto the floor. Unashamed, Ana's eyes traveled over the magnificently built man standing before her. Seeing the evidence of his desire, she suddenly lost her ability to breathe. Her heart wasn't doing very well either, skipping several beats before it began drumming in her chest. Then her eyes locked with his intense gaze as he reached for a towel and wrapped it around his waist. He leaned down to her and whispered, "Don't move, chère. I need to check on Max."

As if she could. She only nodded.

Jake turned and walked to the door. "What is it boy? You hear something?" Max made another whimpering sound and Jake opened the door and followed the dog onto the porch.

A few minutes later, he reappeared along with the dog. "Damn, it's cold out there." He shut the door.

She tried to gather her composure. "What was out there?"

Ana swallowed, gripping hold of her shirt.

He didn't look at her, just walked to the fire and added more wood.

"Jake..."

"No one, Ana. You should go to bed."

He was dismissing her. "Jake, what about what happened between us?"

"Was wrong. It should have never started."

Tears welled in her eyes. "It's what we both want."

He stood and came to her, but didn't touch her. Instead he raked his dark hair away from his face.

"I learned a long time ago," he began. "We can't always have what we want. When I take you back home, I don't want to have to face your family and know that I took advantage of the situation. You're still confused, Ana, and I'm here and handy for you." He touched her face. "But mostly, I don't want you to regret anything that happened between us." His voice lowered. "I couldn't stand that." With that, he walked to the bedroom and closed the door.

Ana sank down on the floor, more alone than ever. Everyone else seemed to know who she was and what was good for her.

All she knew was she was going to lose Jake. Not because he didn't care about her, but because he wanted nothing to do with a princess.

Chapter Nine

Jake shielded his eyes from the sun. Sun?

He raised up on the couch and stared out the window facing east at the bright morning light. He knew the rain had stopped some time during the night because he'd been awake for most of it. But he'd never expected the sunlight this morning.

He tossed aside the blanket, stood, reached for his shirt and slipped it on. He crossed the room in his bare feet, opened the door and stepped out onto the porch. Looking up at the sky, he found lots of blue and a few billowy clouds mixed in. He turned his attention to the ground. There were still puddles, and mud but all in all, it didn't seem too bad.

"Looks pretty good, huh?" He glanced down at Max, who'd followed him out. "A couple days like this one and we could get the truck going and take Ana out of here."

With a forlorn look, the dog started to whine.

"Sorry, fella, she's going home…where she belongs."

Jake was going to miss her, too, but he sure as hell wasn't going to admit it. He thought back to last night, remembering how good she felt in his arms. How sweet she tasted…how badly he wanted her. His body stirred to life, confirming his desire. But from the start it wasn't meant to be; Ana was going to leave. She had to. She didn't belong here—her life was somewhere else.

Did he belong here anymore? Did he really want to stay here…without Ana. He needed to figure out what his plans for the future were going to be.

Over the past two weeks, so much had changed. Ever since one beautiful, stubborn woman had dropped into his life, invaded his space, his thoughts, he'd found himself dreaming about things he never thought he wanted.

Never before had he even considered sharing his life with anyone. Until Ana. She made him painfully aware of everything he'd missed in his solitary life. The closeness, the sharing…the love.

The past two nights, he'd nearly given in to her, but he'd guessed Ana was inexperienced, probably had never been with a man. Yet she'd been willing to give that precious gift to him. That humbled him. No one had ever cared that much. Even if he'd had foolish thoughts about starting something, that all had gotten nixed when he discovered she was a princess. Talk about throwing cold water on a blazing fire….

He had to push aside any hopes he might have because there could be only one option now. To keep Anastasia Penwyck safe and find her a fast exit off the mountain. That wasn't going to be easy. They'd been here nearly two weeks and with the discovery of the diamonds, Jake knew they were in danger. Someone was going to come. He only hoped it was someone from the Penwyck government and not the Black Knights.

Ana didn't want to get out of bed. The rain had stopped. She would be leaving soon. So why wasn't she happy? She probably had a good life on Penwyck. After all, she was a princess. She was more than likely spoiled and had gotten everything her heart desired. None of that mattered to her now. As far as she was concerned, her life had begun the moment Jake Sanderstone found her.

Now, she had to leave him.

There was a knock on the door.

"Go away," she called. After last night, Jake Sanderstone was the last person she wanted to see this morning or any morning.

He felt differently. The door swung open and Ana felt her heart race. He was dressed in his usual attire, faded jeans and a flannel shirt. There was a small nick on his clean shaven jaw.

"Are you ever planning on getting up?" he asked.

"Why? Do I have some pressing engagement?" she grumbled and rolled over. She didn't want him to see that she'd been crying over his rejection. Pity was one thing she didn't need today.

Suddenly the blanket was yanked off her, leaving a lot of her exposed to him. The shirt she'd slept in had ridden up her legs during her restless night.

Under the heat from his intense scrutiny, she fought the urge to squirm. "If you were a gentleman you wouldn't stare.'' She jerked down the shirttail and got some satisfaction from seeing the longing in his eyes.

''After last night, there isn't much either one of us hasn't seen.''

She felt the heat rise to her face.

''Besides, who ever said I was a gentleman?'' He drew a breath and released it slowly. ''And although you are tempting, chère, I have something else in mind, so you might want to get some clothes on.''

''Why? Are you taking me fishing again?''

''We could do that, but I thought you might like to go riding.''

She sat up. ''Riding. Horseback riding? You're really going to take me?''

He shrugged. ''Well, yes, I thought you might like to go with me, but if you'd rather sleep…'' He turned and headed for the door.

''Wait!'' Ana scrambled off the bed and rushed to the door before him, to block his way out. ''You can't leave me here.''

''Says who?''

''Me. I'm a princess…I outrank you.'' She drew herself up straighter. ''And I command you to take me with you.''

He folded his arms over his chest, but his mouth twitched. ''Oh, really?''

She nodded, having trouble looking into his beautiful black eyes. ''Yes.''

''I'm not a citizen of Penwyck so you have no authority over me.''

''Well, ah…as soon as you return me to my country the people will be so grateful to you, they'll…they'll probably make you an honorary citizen.''

"What if I don't want to accept?"

"Oh, but it's such an honor. How could you not?"

He studied her. "You really want to go riding don't you?"

She nodded enthusiastically.

He sighed. "I'll take you. But there are conditions."

"Anything."

"We wait until afternoon so the sun can dry the ground. The terrain is still pretty unstable, but Toby and Maisie are used to this area. In the meantime you can help me muck out the stalls."

She gave him her most endearing smile. "I'd love to. Just allow me a few minutes to dress."

Jake didn't want her dressed, not when there were so many things they could do naked. Slow down, he warned himself, recalling last night and his out of control hormones. No more close calls with this woman, only light and friendly today.

"You have time," he told her. "I meant it when I said we're not going far. But I think we both would feel better doing something besides hanging around the cabin."

She hesitated. "I take it the road down the mountain still isn't safe to travel."

He nodded. "I don't want to chance us getting stuck. If the weather holds, maybe tomorrow."

She lowered her head. "Do you think someone will come up after the diamonds?"

Jake saw her fear and wanted so badly to comfort her. "The chances are slim unless they know the area and have packed mules. Besides, it will be hard to find us. There's a lot of rugged terrain to cover. Now that the weather has cleared, they'll come looking for what they lost. Greed makes people do desperate things. But remember, Princess, a rescue team from Penwyck is searching for you, too. And I won't let anything happen to you, Ana." He hoped he didn't have to prove that.

"I'm not worried, Jake." She smiled, then opened the door. "Now, leave so I can dress." She shoved him out.

He grinned. "You sure are a pushy broad," he teased. Their time together was coming to an end. Today was it. Then Ana would be gone. And he wouldn't have anything to smile about.

Just like before she came.

Ana was tentative as she took Maisie through a few simple commands. Not having ridden the horse before, she wanted to make sure they understood and trusted each other. It didn't take long to learn the animal was gentle and surefooted.

Heading out on the trail, Ana couldn't help but look up at the sky, the sun felt warm and comforting against her face. She didn't need a jacket, but Jake insisted she wear a flannel over her T-shirt. She had on a pair of his jeans, far too big for her. Luckily he had a slim waist and with the aid of his belt, she managed to keep them up. Ahead of her Jake was on Toby. He wasn't what you'd call a natural horseman, but still looked good sitting in the saddle. His posture was erect, his arms relaxed and he had a good seat.

How did she know of these things? Suddenly more knowledge of horses started popping into her mind. Then the picture of children leaning against a paddock fence, cheering her as she rode around. She was seated on the back of a beautiful chestnut roan with a black mane and tail. *Fair Lady!* The horse's name was Fair Lady.

She gasped. Oh, Lord. Lady was her horse. She tried to hold back her panic as she waited for more images. And slowly more came to her. Recognition hit her hard. Along with the children there was a man. He was handsome, with wavy blond hair and kind blue eyes that always held a smile. Rory.

At one time she wanted his love. That youthful infatuation had quickly turned to friendship. Now he was dead.

"Ana, what's wrong?" Jake asked.

"I remembered…I remembered more about Rory. Not only was he my friend, he used to go riding with me." More tears flooded her eyes.

Jake climbed off his horse. He came to her and helped her down. "It's okay, Ana. It's okay."

"You were right," she said, blinking. "I did love him. He was my bodyguard for the past three years. He'd been assigned to me just after I returned home from college." She tried to laugh. "I developed this awful crush on him. I don't know how he put up with it. But Rory never made fun of me, just sternly told me one day that we would be friends—good friends, but nothing more." She laid her head against Jake's chest, needing his strength and warmth. "And we were best friends. Oh, God, he's dead. What am I going to do?"

Jake knew it was terrible to feel jealous over a dead man. But Rory had known Ana for three years. They'd shared so much together. All he'd had was two weeks. "What else do you remember?"

"His smile," she told him. "His kindness. He loved children."

"What children?"

"The children at the orphanage. One day Rory asked me to go with him for a visit, then he convinced me how nice it would be if the kids could learn to ride." Ana raised her head and looked at Jake. "I remember helping him build a training paddock so we would have a place for the lessons."

"That was a pretty nice thing for you to do."

"Rory could talk me into anything. Besides, he'd been raised in an orphanage so he knew how much these kids needed people to care." She shrugged. "I was only helping out. Oh, Jake, what are they going to do without him?"

"They still have you. When you get back, you're going to help them through it. That's why you have to return home."

She nodded. "There are still so many missing pieces to my life."

"Do you remember why you were flying to London?"

She closed her eyes, then a moment later she smiled at being able to remember. "Just what was written in my calendar book, to see the orthopedic surgeon, a Dr. Thor Havenfield. I was going to convince him to see a child at Marlestone House. Catherine. She was six years old and crippled, in the same automobile accident that killed her parents." Ana's eyes grew wide. "Isn't it amazing that I can remember some things but not others."

"Ana, those other memories will come to you."

"Why can't I remember my parents, my sister and brothers?" She shook her head. "Instead I remember my horse." Maisie suddenly gave her a nudge in the back, nearly pushing them over.

"Looks like someone is jealous," Jake said.

Ana turned around and stroked the animal's muzzle and murmured soft words of reassurance.

If you don't feel up to riding, we can return to the cabin," Jake said.

"Not on your life. You promised me a ride…and lunch."

He shook his head. "I never met a woman so set on eating," he teased.

Ana sighed. "I think the fresh air is helping me remember. I love being outside."

"I think it agrees with you, too." Jake touched her face, resisting the urge to kiss her. "You have color in your cheeks." He then picked up Maisie's reins and handed them to her.

He took Toby's and they continued along the trail edged by huge pines. Sun filtered through the tree's branches, casting a dapple light over the rocky hills. The long, wet grass dampened the bottoms of their jeans as they strolled toward the rise and looked out over the lush meadow below. The sky was so blue that it seemed to go on forever.

Ana didn't want to think about what was on the other side. She would forever be haunted by the tragedy of the crash and the good friend she'd lost. Today, she wanted to concentrate on making happy memories of her brief time here with the man she had come to love.

"They call Wales a walking paradise," Jake said. "In this area the trails aren't that easy to maneuver on foot, but the scenery is some of the most beautiful in the world."

They moved a few yards away and Jake took a canvas sheet from his pack and spread it on the ground to protect them from the dampness. Then he placed a blanket over that and set out their lunch: some of Ana's biscuits from last night's dinner and a couple of cans of tuna. They sat and ate in silence, just enjoying the view and being outdoors with each other.

Ana was the one who spoke first. "I wish I could remember more about my life before I return to Penwyck."

"When you see your family, it's bound to trigger something."

"What if it doesn't, Jake?" she asked. "What if I go with these people and never remember who I am?" She looked at him. "I know I've been a lot of trouble for you, but can't you just let me stay a few more days?"

Ana was trouble all right, but not in the way she thought. Jake hated to see her hurting, but he had to send her away. It would be for her own safety.

"Ana, it's not a good idea. No doubt, you have an entire country searching for you. Do you really want to keep your family worrying and wondering if you're dead or alive?"

She shook her head and bit down on her lip. "I shouldn't have asked. You're right of course. And besides you don't need me hanging around, eating up all your food, sleeping in your bed."

He shrugged. "Food is not the problem, chère."

"If I hadn't come along and taken so many of your supplies…"

He pulled her into a rough embrace, making her look at him. "Dammit, Ana. Don't you know that I don't care about the stupid food. You being here with me these past two weeks was the only thing that mattered to me...." He paused as his grip tightened on her.

She put her arms around his waist and held him. They both knew their time together was about over. She would go on with her life, he would go on with his, but nothing would ever be the same.

"Are you trying to tell me you're going to miss me?" she asked.

"Like hell, chère. Like hell," he whispered just before his mouth closed over hers in a searing kiss. She sensed he was trying to relay the feelings he couldn't put into words, but Ana understood them. That was what was breaking her heart.

An hour later, they finished eating lunch. Ana rested against Jake on the blanket, enjoying the warm breeze. In his arms, she felt safe and happy. But it wasn't to last beyond today, this moment. She might love Jake, but she still had to go back to her home.

By late afternoon, the weather turned cool and they packed up their things and started back toward the cabin. After climbing on Maisie, Ana tugged on the reins and headed back toward the trail. When they got to the open meadow she couldn't resist and dug her heels into the horse's sides. Maisie took off running. With the wind in her hair and against her skin, she rode, hard and fast, hoping to clear her head.

All at once, Jake was beside her. "So you want to race?" he yelled, his eyes full of mischief. Then he took off on Toby.

Ana couldn't stand being left behind and urged her mount on. By the time they reached the end of the meadow, both she and Maisie were winded.

Jake helped her down. "We should walk the rest of the way. These guys are probably pretty tired."

Ana was trying to catch her breath. "So am I, but I feel wonderful."

Together they walked the horses the last half mile to the cabin. Once the horses had cooled down, Jake tried to put them back into their stalls. Maisie followed his lead, but Toby refused.

"I guess he likes his freedom too much," Jake said, as he nudged the gelding, but it took a smack on the animal's rump to get him inside. Finally both horses were settled for the night and Ana and Jake headed back to the cabin just as the sun was setting.

"Oh, Jake, look," Ana cried and pointed to the horizon. The orange glow was descending behind the mountains. "No wonder you love it here so much."

Jake came up behind her on the porch. He stood close enough to Ana so that she could feel his breath against her nape, but he didn't touch her. He was already withdrawing from her.

"Do you think the weather will hold through tomorrow?"

"I'm planning on it." He turned her around so she'd have to look at him. "If there was any other way, Ana, you know that I..." He paused. "I want what's best for you."

"I know Jake."

Ana didn't have any idea how hard it was for him to let her go, but he had no choice. If they could make it down the mountain, that meant anyone could get up. The Black Knights weren't going to give up two million dollars worth of diamonds that easily. Jake wanted Ana gone before there was any possibility of trouble. He couldn't let the same thing happen to her as Meg. This time he was going to protect the woman in his care, whether she wanted it or not.

Later that night Ana couldn't sleep. She finally got up, came out of the bedroom and found Jake standing at the window. The fire and the kerosene lantern shed enough light so she could see the breadth of his shoulders covered by a snug-fitting T-shirt. A pair of worn jeans hugged his slim hips and long legs.

"It's going to be a long day tomorrow, you should try and get some sleep," he told her.

"The same holds true for you." She moved further into the room. "Too bad we can't take our own advice. I find myself thinking about my parents. I feel awful for what they've had to go through."

"None of this was your fault. The plane crashed. Besides, I think they'll be overjoyed to see that you're safe."

She thought a minute. "I might have had something to do with it. If the weather was bad, I should have waited, but I bet I talked them into flying. If that's so, then I'm responsible for Rory..."

"Ana..." his warning tone stopped her. "We've gone over this before. The tower cleared the plane for takeoff. They wouldn't have if they thought it wasn't safe."

Jake braced his hands on either side of the window frame and sent up a prayer for another dry day tomorrow. He couldn't handle any more time alone with Ana. She was tempting him beyond belief. The sooner he got her out of his life, the faster he could get her out of his head. But he doubted he'd ever get her out of his heart.

"Jake," she called, her voice soft and inviting. His

body immediately reacted. He drew a breath and released it, but found it difficult with the tightening in his chest.

"Please, look at me, Jake," she asked.

He didn't have much strength left and glanced over his shoulder to find her standing by the hearth. The fire light created a mellow glow all around her. Her light brown hair was soft and wavy, streaming down to her shoulders. Her beauty was only enhanced by her brilliant blue eyes.

Jake wanted her so badly he ached...everywhere. His fingers itched to touch her, to caress her flawless skin, kiss her and bring her pleasure. But he had no right. She would leave tomorrow. And he had to find a way to survive without her.

"Ana...it would be a good idea if you went back to bed. At least try and sleep."

"I don't want to be alone. Not tonight."

"Are you worried about someone coming while we're asleep?"

She started across the room. "No, I'm not worried. I just don't want to be without...you."

He felt his heart pounding in his chest. "Ana, we talked about this before—"

"No, *you* talked about it. I never got to vote." She stopped in front of him. "I'm leaving tomorrow, Jake. Is it so difficult to talk with me?"

"If I felt that way, I wouldn't have spent the day with you."

"Then why, when we returned to the cabin did you run me off to bed?"

He hated her choice of words. "Because when you're around, especially at night, we seem to get into trouble."

"Didn't we have fun today?"

"Yeah, we did."

"Then what is different now?"

"You can't be that naive, Ana. I can't keep my hands off you."

She smiled. "I like that you feel that way."

"Well, I don't," he chided. "So go back to bed."

"No, I want to talk," she said stubbornly.

"What do you want to talk about?"

She took hold of his hand and led him to the couch. "I want to carry on a normal conversation with you. And I want the truth."

She pushed him down on the cushion, then sat next to him, tucking her feet under her. She was too close.

"Are you going to live up here through the winter months?"

"I haven't decided," he told her truthfully.

"Are you going back to the FBI?"

He frowned. "If you're worried I'll go hungry, don't. I made good money over the years and invested well."

"I'm worried about you being up here all alone. No one to take care of you." She brushed back his hair.

"Don't be," he murmured, but didn't pull away. "I've been alone all my life."

"I don't even know where you live."

"Here."

"Besides here. Do you have a home in the States?"

Home. Had he ever had a home? "I have a small house in New Orleans, in the garden district."

"I bet it's lovely."

"It needs a lot of work. I've never had enough time to start any renovations." And no one cared if he did.

"I would like to see it one day. Maybe if I get to New Orleans…"

"Sure," he said.

Ana's gaze sought his. There was so much loneliness in those dark depths. She leaned over and kissed him, nothing serious, just a peck against the mouth. Then she ducked down laid her head in Jake's lap. When he didn't resist, she placed her hand on his thigh. "You're not alone, Jake. You have me now."

For a long time, he didn't say anything. Then his hand began to stroke her back.

"Jake, if you ever find you need me, promise you'll get in touch with me. That is, if you want to."

"I'll just call the palace on Penwyck, right? Ask for Princess Anastasia."

She could hear the humor in his voice, but it brought tears to her eyes. No matter how much he needed her, she would probably never see or hear from him again.

"Of course," she said. "There's probably a switchboard, or I can find out the private number and give it to you."

"How can you call me when I don't have a phone here?"

"I thought maybe you would be going back to New Orleans."

"I'm not sure what my plans are."

Her heart pounded in her chest, like a pendulum reminding her that their time together was running out.

"Jake…I know, you don't do commitments. That you've always been by yourself. And you don't have to worry that I'll annoy you or expect anything from you.'' She rolled over to look up at him. ''I just want you to know that…I love you, Jake Sanderstone.''

His dark eyes locked with hers. His breathing grew rapid as he reached down and lifted her into his arms. ''Why did you have to go and say that? Don't you know that I'm the last person you should love?''

''You're wrong, Jake. You're the only person I can love.''

He shut his eyes. ''That doesn't change anything, chère. I still have to let you go.''

Chapter Ten

A knock sounded on Colonel Pierce Prescott's office door. He looked up from his desk to see Captain Millner.

"Yes, captain."

"Sir, Colonel Harper just reported in. They've located Royal Bird Two's crash site."

"It's taken a bloody long time." Pierce stood and tossed his pen on his desk. He didn't want to ask the next question, but there wasn't a choice. "Are there any survivors?"

"We're not sure, sir. The only verification is the location of the plane. The area is remote, but according to one of the locals, there's a cabin not far from the site. There's hope that the owner, an American named Jake Sanderstone, saw the plane go down and went to help."

"I assume that no one's been in contact with this man."

"No sir, there's no telephone in his cabin, and with the storm, he must have been stranded, too."

"Outstanding." Pierce moved around his desk, praying this American was able to help. "Do we have any idea who this Sanderstone is?"

"The Intelligence report states that he was an FBI agent for twelve years, but the rest of his file is inaccessible to us."

Pierce knew that could mean several things. The man could still work for the agency, his job was classified.

"Sir, there's also been another development."

He didn't like the captain's anxious look. "What?"

"We've discovered that the man who was piloting the princess's plane is Stephen Loden."

The name wasn't familiar to him. "Am I supposed to know this man?"

"No, sir, but we've learned that Loden's a member of his rebel group, the Black Knights."

The colonel began to pace as rage churned through him. "Bloody hell. Was this another kidnapping attempt?"

"No sign of that, sir. But we do believe that Loden was smuggling stolen diamonds out of the country. There's been a theft at the mine. We didn't connect the two at first, but it makes sense. The plane had diplomatic clearance, and with the princess along, there wouldn't be any customs search at the airport."

Pierce clenched his fists. He wanted nothing more than to get Broderick alone for about thirty minutes. But he couldn't think about taking revenge now. More than likely the Black Knights were looking for the downed plane and the contraband. He doubted the princess had survived, but if she had, they wouldn't want any witnesses when they came for the diamonds.

The Rangers had to get there first. "When is the team set to deploy?" the colonel asked.

"By dawn."

"Good, put me aboard."

"Yes, sir. Is there anything you need me to do for you?"

Pierce had to make his own preparations. First, he had to tell the queen about the new developments. There hadn't been any good news to begin with, now it was looking worse. But he couldn't give her any false hope, either. Realistically, he knew there wouldn't be any survivors.

Penwyck's monarch had had more than her share to deal with of late, and he wanted to let her know that he was prepared take some of the burden.

"I promised the queen that I would bring her daughter home. And by God, I'm going to do it. We're getting to that plane first. Tell the crew to expect me at 0500 hours and be ready to take off. There will be no delays!"

Ana called out his name, pleading with him to help her. Jake tried but he was being held down by two men as a third man grabbed Ana and dragged her away. She fought him, but was overpowered by the kidnapper's strength and unable to get free.

Jake continued to struggle. He was the only one who could save her, but he got gut-punched for his efforts. Even doubled over in pain, he worked to break their hold on his arms.

Dammit, he couldn't let it happen again. He

*couldn't let them take Ana. He promised her he would
keep her safe.*

"Please, help me, Jake," Ana cried.

*With the last of his strength, he raised his leg and
kicked his attacker, sending him backward, then hit
the other man between the eyes. Suddenly free, Jake
charged after Ana's captor. When he reached them,
the man released Ana to fight him off.*

"Run Ana..." He cried. "Run."

"Jake! Jake, wake up."

He woke up with a gasp and sucked air into his
oxygen starved lungs. His heart was pounding like a
drum. Blinking to adjust his eyes to the dim room, he
turned to the woman next to him on the couch. Ana.

He grabbed her and pulled her against him. "Thank
God. You're safe."

"Yes, I'm safe. It was only a dream."

He inhaled the scent of her sweet smelling hair and
reveled in the feel of her soft body. "God, I
thought..."

She leaned back and looked at him. Even in the
pale light, he could see she'd been asleep. "You
thought what?"

"Nothing." He drew her back into his arms.

"Jake, it wasn't nothing."

Seeing the blanket wrapped around them, he realized that she'd never gone to bed. She'd fallen asleep
beside him. He'd never slept with anyone. If he'd
spent time with women, he never stayed the night.

But now, he couldn't imagine ever letting her go.

"It was just a bad dream," he said. "I have them
all the time. One of the hazards of my job."

He wasn't about to tell her of his premonition. He
had to make sure he got her out of harm's way and

that meant he had to get her off the mountain at first light.

"Go back to sleep. It'll be morning soon enough." And he would have to let her go, he told himself.

God help him, he had to find a way to let her leave him.

The sun was streaming through the window, causing Ana to squint. She raised up but found herself trapped in Jake's arms on the small couch. Somehow during the night, he'd stretched out beside her. Not a bad place to be. She smiled. Laying her head back down, she snuggled closer to him.

He groaned, then murmured something into her hair. Ana inhaled his familiar scent and placed her cheek against his solid chest. No matter what happened in the future, she'd never regret this time with Jake. Even though they'd never actually made love, they'd shared so much. Feeling her emotions surfacing, she closed her eyes. Sobs bubbled up in her throat. How could she say goodbye?

"You promised," Jake said, his voice husky. "You wouldn't cry."

"Who says I'm crying?" She wiped away her tears and looked at him. "I just have something in my eyes."

"You may be good at poker, chère, but you're lousy at lying." His dark eyes bore into hers. "We've talked about this Ana. It's time. We need to go…now."

"I know." She sat up. "I'll get dressed and feed Toby and Maisie."

"No, I'll do it." He stood and stretched, then walked to the door and stepped into his boots. She loved watching him, even doing mundane things, like putting on his shirt. But her joy turned to fear when he picked up his gun, reached behind him and tucked it into the waistband of his jeans.

"What's the gun for?"

"Just a precaution." He was out the door before she could ask any more questions.

Thirty minutes later, Ana sat at the table trying to eat, but she couldn't get the food past the lump in her throat. Jake wasn't eating, either. Silently, she washed up the dishes, then helped Jake gather some things he needed for the trip, including the bag of stolen diamonds. He stashed them under the front seat of the truck.

"Pray that this old baby gets us down the mountain," Jake said.

Ana bit down on her lower lip as she fought her tears.

"Come on, chère. It isn't safe here. I need to get you home to your family."

With a nod, Ana went back to the cabin and looked around, but she had nothing to take with her. Her clothes were in shreds. She had on Jake's jeans and shirt and a pair of beat-up canvas shoes. Would her family even recognize her when she showed up?

Earlier she'd gone out to the shed and said goodbye to Toby and Maisie. How could she care so much about some silly horses? But she did. And Max. She owed the dog her life. He'd led Jake to the plane, and to her.

"You ready?" Jake called to her.

Never. She'd never be ready to leave. Everything she wanted was here. She nodded, then walked with him to the truck when the sound of a vehicle coming up the road stopped them. Finally, a late model Range Rover came into view.

Jake's body tensed as it went on alert for danger. Immediately, he stepped in front of Ana. "Go inside," he ordered her.

"But Jake…"

"Go inside the cabin, Ana, until I find out who they are."

Three men climbed out of the vehicle, all dressed in black jumpsuits. Over the left breast was the Penwyck crest. More importantly to Jake were the guns holstered at their waist.

"Princess Anastasia, you're alive," one of the men called when he spotted Ana. He bowed then started toward her.

Jake reached for his gun and pulled it out. "Just hold it right there, gentlemen. I need to see some identification first.

"My God, man. We should be the ones asking for identification. Do you realize who this woman is?"

Jake nodded. "I do. And that's the reason I'm taking precautions."

When the leader saw that Jake wasn't going to back down, he pulled a plastic military ID from his pocket and handed it to him. It identified Captain Ben Trent from the Royal Navy SEALs.

Everything looked on the up-and-up, but something still didn't feel right to Jake. He lowered his gun and slipped it into the front of his jeans as he eyed the three men, not liking the odds. If he had to, he could take out two of them, but the third would be a problem.

"I'm Jake Sanderstone, FBI," he lied. "I know

I'm out of my jurisdiction, but the princess was in need of a temporary bodyguard.''

"The princess is the only survivor of the crash?''

Jake nodded. "Ana,'' he called over his shoulder. "Do you recognize any of these men?''

"No,'' she said.

It was Ben Trent who spoke, "The princess and I have never officially met. I have never been assigned to the palace or the royal family.''

Jake wondered what exactly were these men's duties. "I would think that the Penwyck government would send more than three men to search for their princess.''

Trent looked nervous. Not so much that the average person could notice, but Jake saw his jaw twitch. "I have to insist that you release the princess,'' Trent said. "The king and queen have been terribly distraught since the crash.''

"I'm not holding the princess,'' Jake insisted. "She's been here because we've been unable to get down the mountain.''

Ana walked to Jake's side. "Have you been in touch with my family?''

The men exchanged glances, then one reached in his suit's zipper pocket and took out his ID. "Yes, Your Royal Highness.'' He bowed and handed her his card. "The queen is worried. The whole country is in mourning, thinking you perished in the crash.''

Curt Johnson was the man's name, Jake noted, unable to shake the uneasy feeling. Was it personal, or was there really something wrong here? He still wasn't convinced they were sent by the Royal Elite Team.

"I might have died, but Jake found me and brought me back here."

"Can you tell us what happened?"

Ana shook her head. Everything was so confusing. "I haven't been able to remember much since the accident."

Ben glanced from Ana to Jake. "What do you mean? Your memory is gone?"

Jake didn't like Ana giving away so much information. "She's gotten a lot of it back."

"Do you remember what caused the accident?"

"I hadn't remembered any of the crash until yesterday," she said. "But I believe it was the weather. Rory's last words were that they were going to try and land the plane."

"Do you think you could take us back to the plane?"

"I could," she said, her back straightened. "But Jake would be better able to get you there. Besides, I have no desire to go back."

Jake stepped in. "I think our first priority is to get the princess home. You can bring a team back to go over the crash site."

"I'm afraid we can't wait that long." Curt suddenly reached out and took hold of Ana.

Jake reacted at the same time, but the other two men grabbed him. He was fighting them off when he heard Ana scream. He whistled for Max, and the dog immediately jumped Johnson, the man holding Ana, and he was forced to release her.

"Run, Ana. Get the hell out of here." Jake took another punch in the jaw that sent him backward, but he countered with a roundhouse kick that drove Trent to the ground.

With only seconds to recover, Jake ordered Max to go after Ana, then dove after his gun, but had it kicked away before he could reach it.

Jake used his martial arts training, but these men were just as skilled in combat. He managed to get in a few licks. He grabbed Trent's collar where he discovered the black sword tattoo. It didn't take long before the rebels had Jake outnumbered and subdued.

"You're going to be sorry for this." Trent said as he pulled a gun and aimed it at Jake's head. Jake didn't care about his own life, he just prayed that Ana had gotten away and found a place to hide until help arrived.

"Don't shoot him, yet," Curt yelled. "He's going to lead us to the plane."

"Like hell," Jake taunted, then got a kick in the gut for his wise mouth.

"You will, or we're going to hunt down the princess." Trent gave him a sinister smile. "And then we'll have a little fun. Perhaps you'll be willing to talk now."

They yanked Jake to his feet just as he heard a sound from overhead. Helicopters. One...two...no, four were coming over the ridge. The men released Jake, ran for the Range Rover and raced off down the road.

Unable to land, the helicopters hovered overhead as a rope ladder was dropped out the side and rangers climbed down to the ground. Several of the men ran off toward the vehicle.

Another ran toward him. Jake recognized the colonel's insignia on his jumpsuit. "I'm Colonel Pierce Prescott, Penwyck Army. These men are Royal Rangers. Are you all right, Mr. Sanderstone?"

Jake nodded as he wiped the blood from his swollen lip. "I don't have time for the niceties, Colonel," he yelled over the sound of the rotor blades. "Ana is out there by herself."

The man looked confused. "Ana? You mean Anastasia? She's alive?"

"That's exactly what I'm saying. I sent her off when the Black Knights showed up."

By a handheld radio, the Colonel gave orders for two of the helicopters to track down the Range Rover. Jake was already on his way up the ridge. He wasn't sure in what direction Ana had gone, but he was sure he was going to find her.

Twenty minutes later, a trembling Ana huddled in the grove of pines. Somehow she'd made the climb to the crash site, knowing that Jake would have to bring the men here.

She didn't want to run off, but Jake had made her go. What were they going to do to him? Oh, God! What if they'd killed him because of those stupid diamonds?

Ana glanced around the debris. She had to find some kind of a weapon. She suddenly remembered that while Rory had carried a gun holstered under his suit jacket, he also had a reserve in his bag. She ran to the midsection and went inside. The sight of the twisted metal triggered her memory, nearly making her sick. She pushed aside the horrific flashback, knowing she couldn't let anyone else die. She hurried to the bench seat and pried open the bent lid. When she finally was able to lift it, she found Rory's travel bag.

Ana pulled it out and began digging through the

clothes. Her breath caught when she came in contact with the cold metal. With a shaky hand, she drew out the pistol, then reached back in the bag for the magazine. She checked to find a full clip, then clicked it into place.

She inhaled a deep, long breath, hoping to give her strength. "Come on, Max, we need to find a place to hide…and wait." She glanced toward the graves, silently thanking Rory, not just for the gun, but for teaching her how to shoot it.

She hid behind the trees, facing the trail. She wanted to make sure she had a good view. Her father had taught her to face her enemies, not run from them. "Or you'll be running all your life…" she whispered the familiar words as if they were a prayer. They were from King Morgan Penwyck.

A smile broke through her terror. She remembered. Her father was sick. He was in a coma, fighting for his life. A tear rolled down her face as more memories flooded her head. Her mother was beautiful Queen Marissa. Megan, her sister, was married and expecting a child. With each acknowledgment, Ana's excitement grew. Meredith, who would be married soon, too. And she had two brothers, Owen and Dylan. She gasped, recalling the kidnapping attempt on her sibling. "Mother must be so frightened about me."

More tears escaped her eyes as she thought about never going back to Penwyck, never seeing her family. She wiped them away, to clear her vision. Jake said she needed to take care of the kids at the orphanage.

Oh, Jake. Where are you?

A strength she never knew she had erupted within her. No, she wasn't going to let these men do this.

She couldn't let them take everything away from her. The Black Knights were trying to destroy her family. "Come, Max. Jake needs us."

The dog barked and followed after his mistress. She hadn't gotten very far when she heard her name being called.

"Ana! Ana! Where are you?"

"Jake! Jake, I'm over here."

Max barked and ran off just as Jake appeared over the ridge. Crying and stumbling through the brush, Ana finally ended up in his arms.

"Thank, God. You're safe." He pulled her tighter.

"I am now," she said. "Since you're here. I was so afraid…" She drew back and examined his battered face. "Oh, Jake, you're hurt."

"It's nothing." He shrugged. "Oh, God, Ana, I thought…if they'd gotten you…" His dark eyes locked with hers. He was unable to hide his concern or how much he cared for her. Then as if realizing what he was doing, he glanced down at the gun in her belt.

"Where did this come from?"

"It's Rory's," she explained. "I remembered he kept an extra gun in his bag."

He slipped it from her jeans. "I don't think you're going to need it now. Reinforcements have arrived. Didn't you hear the helicopters?"

She shook her head. "I've been too busy, running."

"You don't have to run anymore, Princess Anastasia." The familiar voice caused her to turn around.

Ana blinked at the man, then recognition hit her. "Pierce. Is that you?"

The dark haired man grinned. "I thought I better come after you myself. Your mother is worried."

Ana went running into the man's arms. "Oh, Pierce, I'm so glad to see you."

Jake wanted to beat the man to a pulp.

"Looks like you got yourself into some trouble," Pierce said. "But you managed to survive."

"The plane went down in the bad weather. It was Jake and Max who found me. And I wouldn't have endured if he hadn't taken care of me."

"I didn't do that much, just got her out of the elements. She had a slight concussion."

"But Rory died…" Ana said, her voice sad. "He made sure I was well padded for the crash. Jake buried him and the pilot under the tree."

"He was a good man," the colonel acknowledged.

"I want to bring Rory back home, Pierce. I think he would want to be buried at Marlestone House."

"Of course. It may take a few days, but we'll take him home, Ana."

Pierce took one look at Sanderstone and recognized the man's jealousy. And after witnessing the searing looks between the two, the colonel didn't doubt that something had happened during their isolation and it sure as hell wasn't platonic.

"Well, the first thing we have to do is let your mother know you are safe." Pierce visually checked Ana. Her hair was a mess. She was dressed in baggy jeans and shirt. He laughed. "You look like a waif, but I'm sure the queen will take you any way she can get you."

Ana turned to Jake. "Oh, Jake, we're safe and we're going home."

He shook his head. "No, Princess, you're going home where you belong. I'm staying here."

"Surely you'll come back with me just for a few days," she said. "Meet my family. My father and mother."

The colonel spoke. "Why don't I let you two have a little privacy?" He walked back to the wreckage and talked with one of his men.

Jake turned to Ana. He saw the pain and hurt in her eyes and had to look away. This was going to be harder than he'd thought, but it was best for everyone.

"Look, Ana. We both knew this was going to happen. That you'd be rescued and return home."

"But…I thought…when the time came you would decide that we belonged together."

It had been Jake's dream, too. But that's all it was. A dream. "Do you really think I'd fit into your lifestyle? I am a commoner and you're royalty. I wear flannel shirts and faded jeans. I drink beer and drive a truck."

"You also love horses and dogs." She moved closer to him. "But none of that matters if you care about me."

He puffed out a breath. This was killing him. "You want a home and family. I don't do that." He'd stopped wishing for that years ago.

"Oh, Jake. You do could those things best of all, if only you would trust."

He couldn't let himself weaken. He needed to send her away. "I learned to trust myself. In the long run, that's all I've had to depend on."

"You could depend on me."

"You're high-maintenance. Our lifestyles are so far apart, Princess."

"We managed to get along these past two weeks."

"I've been up here a long time." His gaze went to her mouth. "And you were pretty tempting. But if I need a woman to warm my bed, there are a lot of them out there that don't want a commitment."

Ana's face flushed. "I didn't realize I was so much trouble."

Jake wanted to take all the cruel words back. He clenched his fists, fighting to keep her from convincing him into believing they could make it.

"I guess I better leave then. I've already overstayed my welcome." She started to walk away, then stopped. "Just one more thing, Jake." Ana stepped toward him and slipped her arms around his neck. She raised up on her tiptoes and placed her mouth against his.

Jake tried to resist, but he couldn't. With a groan, he jerked her against him and deepened the kiss. He savored the softness of her body, her heart beating with his. His tongue moved against her teeth, then slipped inside to taste her sweetness one more time. For the last time.

Finally he released her. Seeing her mouth wet and swollen from their shared passion, he nearly reached for her again.

"You're just going to let me go?" she whispered, her voice shaky.

Dammit, didn't she realize this was for the best. "You were never mine to keep, chère."

"I've never been any man's but yours Jake. And no other woman will love you the way I do."

He was dying. "You only think you love me, Princess. In a few days you'll forget this ordeal."

She smiled and his heart tripped. "I will never forget you, Jake. Just like you'll never forget me. And I dare you to try.'' Tears suddenly welled in her eyes. "Goodbye, Jake.''

She turned and walked steadily toward the colonel. Then Prescott put his arm around her shoulder and began their journey back to her past life.

One of the rangers came toward Jake. "Sir. We have a medic aboard the helicopter to look at your wounds.''

"I'm fine,'' Jake answered. "It's just some cuts and bruises.''

"You could have internal injuries, sir.''

He had internal injuries all right, but nothing a doctor could fix. He looked on silently as Ana disappeared from his view…and his life.

But never from his heart.

Chapter Eleven

Ana rode Fair Lady along the deserted beach, the chestnut thoroughbred kicking up sand beside the water's edge. The sea breeze was unseasonably warm and felt good against her skin as it blew her hair from her face. And for a short time, during the early morning ride, Ana forgot her misery. But even being atop Lady hadn't given her the solace she once had. When life was simpler.

It had been a week since Ana returned home. The loneliest week of her life. Most of her memory had returned and she had tried to go on with her life as usual, but what was once normal was no more. Going to Marlestone House without Rory had been the hardest thing she'd ever done. The second hardest had been explaining to the children he wasn't coming back.

She found it hard to believe that her friend was gone. Who could she talk to? Her sisters were involved in their lives, one expecting a child, the other preparing for a wedding.

Her father was still in a coma. She prayed every night that he would get better. Since her return to Penwyck, she and her mother had grown closer, but she hadn't been able to confide in her, or anyone, about Jake.

Ana tugged on the reins and slowed Lady to a walk to cool her down. The animal reared back, wanting to race again. Her thoughts went to Maisie and Toby and she smiled, wondering if they missed her. Was Jake taking good care of them? And how would they all manage to survive the winter in the mountains? How would Jake survive?

Anger rose within her and she hoped he was as miserable as she. Swinging her leg over the horse, she jumped to the sand. "Stubborn man," she hissed. "He doesn't know what's good for him."

"Most men don't."

Ana turned around to find her mother walking toward her. "Mother, I didn't see you."

"I don't think you've seen much these days."

Queen Marissa was a beautiful woman. Even dressed in slacks and a sweater, with her hair pulled away from her face, she looked years younger than her age. "I know your ordeal was horrific, Anastasia. I also wonder if you're telling us everything. Pierce told me about your Mr. Sanderstone—"

"He's not mine." She rubbed Lady's muzzle. "What did he say about Jake?"

"Not much, but as your mother, I was concerned about you being alone with a stranger for weeks."

"No need to worry, Mother, Jake was a perfect

gentleman." Tears filled her eyes. "Very much the gentleman."

Marissa smiled gently. "That is reassuring. But I have a feeling that you and this man have...formed a closeness."

Ana studied her mother. "Not as close as I would have liked."

Her mother nodded as if she understood. "Are you saying you're in love with Jake Sanderstone?"

Just mention of Jake's name brought Ana pain. But she couldn't hold her feelings in any longer. "Yes, mother that's what I'm saying. But a great lot of good it's doing me. The man couldn't wait to get rid of me." Tears flooded her eyes, then spilled down her face.

Marissa drew her daughter into her arms. She knew how hard it was for Anastasia to admit any weakness. A trait she had definitely inherited from her father.

As for Mr. Sanderstone wanting to get rid of Anastasia, the queen knew differently. The man had risked his life for her daughter. That alone made him special in her eyes. Pierce himself had witnessed a kiss exchanged between them, and the possessive look in the man's eyes when he had to let Anastasia go.

"Maybe the reason Mr. Sanderstone let you go is because he cares so much. And you are a princess. That in itself can be a little overwhelming."

"But that shouldn't stop a person if he truly loves someone."

"Darling, you are talking about a man here. A prideful man."

Marissa's first concern had always been her children and their happiness. She'd been lucky enough to have made a love match in her marriage to the king. And she wanted the same for each of her sons and daughters.

Maybe it was time to test her theory she had on Mr. Sanderstone. To see for herself just how much he cared for Anastasia.

After all it was her right as queen…and mother.

A week later, two military escorts arrived and drove Jake down the mountain to a waiting helicopter and flew him to the island. From overhead, he saw the incredible beauty of Penwyck with the green mountain range and the long white sandy beaches.

It looked like paradise.

Jake didn't want to come to Penwyck. It had been Colonel Prescott who had strongly persuaded him that the Royal Elite Team needed to confer with him again about the plane crash, and what took place with the Black Knights.

He wanted to help as much as possible to stop these rebels but they'd questioned him thoroughly that day. During the past week, a team of men had been sent to the crash site to gather information. They'd carefully exhumed the two bodies he'd buried and took them back to Penwyck.

Truth was, he liked the distraction, but it only helped for the days, the nights, the long lonely nights, he only had his own company and all he could think about was Ana. How much he missed her and that was why he couldn't stay in the cabin any longer. So, just as soon as he finished another round of answering questions, he was headed back to the States.

Jake needed to move on with his life, he just hadn't figured out how. What were his options? He could go into the private sector as an investigator, or he could go back to the bureau. His superior had always said he'd had a job there. One thing Jake knew, he didn't want that solitary life again.

After four hours with the Royal Elite Team, Jake was impressed with the thoroughness of the interrogation. He wouldn't have been surprised if they'd asked him to strip down and show any birthmarks he had. Finally they called a halt to the proceedings and thanked him for his cooperation.

Glad it was over, Jake just wanted to head home. The last thing he needed was to run into Ana, although, he was somewhat surprised that he hadn't seen her. Why should she hang around even if she knew he was going to be here? He'd told her to get on with her life, just like he planned to do.

A uniformed guard dressed in black trousers and a red double-breasted jacket adorned with a white sash led him into the great hall. The country's flag, red with a white border and crossed gold sabers in the center, hung on one wall.

Jake looked around at the rich tapestries on the walls, the imported marble flooring and the high, hand-painted ceilings. On another wall he spotted a portrait of the royal family. The king and queen and their five children. His chest tightened as he examined the beautiful woman who had stolen two weeks of his life, along with his heart. Hell, he had to get out of here. Now.

He checked his watch. If he left now, he could get back to the cabin by nightfall.

"Do you need to be somewhere, Jake?"

Jake turned around to find Colonel Prescott. "Just

have to get back before dark. I have animals who depend on me."

"Not to worry, there are two men watching the cabin and tending to Max and the horses."

"Your people are thorough."

"We just wanted to show our appreciation for all you've done for Ana."

"I told you I don't want any medals."

Pierce grinned. "I assure you, Jake, the queen isn't going to give you one. Just her thanks." The colonel raised an eyebrow. "She requested to see you for a few minutes in the rose garden." He led Jake down a long hallway that displayed beautiful antiques, the walls adorned with several paintings. Jake knew enough about art to recognize the work of famous artists.

"As an ex-FBI agent," the colonel began, "what would you think about working with RET?"

"It's not exactly my style."

"You might be surprised how well you could adapt."

"I doubt I would fit in."

"I didn't think I would either."

Jake raised an eyebrow. "Since you hold the title of duke, that's a little hard to believe."

Pierce grew serious. "I was awarded the title for my military service. I'm a commoner like you. My father was a minister, my mother a schoolteacher. Not all of us are born into royalty, but that isn't stopping me from marrying a princess." He grinned. "I'm engaged to Ana's sister, Meredith."

Prescott's announcement caught Jake off guard. Suddenly he found himself thinking about a possible chance for him and Ana. He looked around, unable to imagine he could ever fit in here. He'd never fit in anywhere before, but with Ana, it had been different. Damn, he missed her so much. He couldn't resist asking, "How is Ana…I mean the princess, doing?"

The colonel gave him a sideways glance. "I'd say she's doing about as well as you are."

Without any more explanation, he led Jake through the large plate glass doors into the garden. Flashes of brilliant colors struck him first, then an intoxicating fragrance. Elegant statues of maidens stood regally among the rows of perfect roses. Fountains spouted water out of cherubs' mouths and splashed into a pond below where colorful Koi swam. All was surrounded by ten-foot high walls, protecting this private place.

A beautiful woman appeared under a vine-covered lattice gazebo. She had nearly black hair and sparkling blue eyes. She was dressed in a flowing black skirt and ivory silk blouse. She smiled sweetly and Jake knew instantly she was Ana's mother.

He bowed awkwardly. "Your Majesty."

"Mr. Sanderstone. So nice to finally meet you." She held out her hand.

He took it. "It's my pleasure."

"No, it's mine to be able to thank the man who was instrumental in returning my daughter to me. I know you jeopardized your own life to keep Anastasia from harm."

"I just took a few hits, the bruises are nearly gone."

"And then you had to be subjected to more. I hope the RET weren't too brutal in their interview. I'm sure you understand it's for national security."

"I understand completely," Jake said. "Besides,

my skin is pretty thick. I only hope my cooperation will help bring these men to justice."

"We seem to have a problem with that," the colonel stepped closer. "That's why we brought you here, Jake. Your credentials are impeccable and your experience with the FBI would be vital to help with our cause. We were hoping we could persuade you to take on the challenge and join our team."

Jake had no idea that he would be offered anything. But how could he think about a job that would keep him close to Ana. "I appreciate the offer, but I don't think it's such a good idea."

"If it's a question of money, you will be compensated well," the queen said.

"No, it's not about money, Your Majesty."

She raised an eyebrow obviously, expecting an explanation for his refusal.

"I doubt your daughter would be too happy to have me around."

The queen looked him in the eye. "I haven't discussed this with Anastasia. In fact, she has no idea you are here. In all honesty, I wanted to meet you myself and find out what intrigued my daughter so." She smiled, but didn't say any more, only checked her watch. "If you'll excuse me, I have pressing matters to attend to."

She turned to the colonel. "Pierce, I've decided to send Amira to New York to meet with Marcus Cordello. Now, don't argue, I've already made the arrangements. I feel this is going to take a woman's touch to get this job done. And I need to put an end to any doubt about my sons."

She sighed, then turned back to Jake.

"So there are no misunderstandings, the Royal

Elite Team does not offer positions as a gesture of thanks.'' She studied him for a moment. ''Your reluctance surprises me, Jake. May I call you Jake?''

He nodded. ''Please.''

''I took you as a man who is open to new challenges. I could be wrong, of course. Maybe you and Ana should talk before you leave.''

Jake blinked. ''Ana and I said our goodbyes on the mountain.''

''Maybe that is just as well. Anastasia is going to be angry knowing we were discussing her.'' She looked at the colonel. ''Pierce, I will talk with you later.''

The men bowed, waited until the queen disappeared, then Prescott turned to Jake.

''So you're just going to walk away from Ana, knowing she's in love with you.''

Jake didn't want to but it was for the best. ''You don't understand. I wouldn't fit in here.''

The colonel looked unconvinced. ''You could if you truly wanted to.''

Oh, he wanted to, so bad he could taste it. They were dangling everything he'd ever wanted in his face. ''I've never fit in many places.''

''Stop feeling sorry for yourself, Sanderstone. I already know about your past, the good and the bad. You managed to get out of the slums and leave your horrendous childhood behind. You put yourself through school and worked your way up through the ranks of the FBI.''

Jake tried to hide his surprise, but failed.

''Do you have any idea what an honor it is to be asked to join the RET? And by the queen herself?

Just in case you didn't read between the lines, she was giving you her permission to pursue Anastasia.''

A huge ache settled in Jake's chest. "I didn't ask her to.''

"Enough with the bloody attitude. The princess will arrive here shortly. If you're fool enough to walk out of her life, please let her down gently. But if you're as smart as I think you are, you won't walk away.'' Prescott turned and marched off.

The colonel was right, Jake wanted it all. The new start, a place to call home and the love of a woman. All he had to do to get it was risk his heart.

Jake heard a sound and turned to see Ana walk through the garden. She was as incredibly beautiful as he remembered. Her hair was all soft and flowing. She'd had it trimmed to her shoulders and pulled away from her face. Only a touch of makeup was needed to enhance her already striking features, especially those incredible eyes.

Ana had on a light gauzy dress with small blue flowers. Heat surged through him as his gaze moved over the fitted bodice, then along the flowing skirt that ended just below her knees. Next came his favorite part, her gorgeous legs. Long, shapely calves and trim ankles that ended with her slender feet encased in a pair of strappy high heels. He was dying.

She looked up and saw him. "Jake…''

"Hello, AnP—rincess.''

"I had no idea you would be here.''

Ana should have been furious with her mother for doing this, but after seeing Jake she was so grateful.

"I just finished talking with Queen Marissa and Colonel Prescott. I was about to leave.''

She couldn't seem to stop looking at him. His hair

was short, but still covered his ears. He wore khaki pants and brown loafers. A suit jacket hung open revealing a light blue shirt with the collar, open. He'd had on a tie earlier, but it was gone now. His face was clean shaven and she noticed another nick on his chin. His eyes were still mesmerizing, and as dark and deep as onyx. She was so angry with the man, and so in love.

"Don't let me keep you." She pointed to the back wall. "There's a gate that leads out of here. Ask a guard for directions to Pierce's office. I'm sure he'll make arrangements for you to return to Wales."

One, two…three heart beats passed and Jake hadn't moved. "I've missed you," he said.

Ana shook her head, not wanting to hear he'd missed her, but didn't have room for her in his life. "Please, Jake. Don't. You said everything you wanted when I left the mountain. Just go back to your cabin and have a happy life." She turned away, hoping he'd leave, praying he'd stay.

He walked up behind her. "I was thinking about selling it."

Shocked, she swung around. "No! You can't. You love it there."

Jake glanced away. "It's not the same."

Ana saw something in his eyes and she tentatively moved closer. "Why isn't it the same, Jake?"

He drew a breath. "Dammit, you're not there. That's why."

A thrill raced through her. "Was that so hard to say?"

"Oh, Ana…" He shook his head and reached for her hand. She gasped as if it were her lifeline. And it had once been exactly that.

"I have no idea why I'm here. Ana, you deserve better than someone used up by life. Someone who's seen what I've seen and been where I've been."

"Then why did you stay to see me, Jake?" A tear escaped down her cheek as she waited for him to say the words she needed to hear.

His eyes held hers. "I thought I could leave, but I can't. For the first time in my life, I'm afraid—afraid I can't give you what you want, what you need." He swallowed. "Dammit! I've never been good at relationships."

She wanted to rush into his arms, but held her ground. "There's only one thing I need from you, Jake." They both knew what that was. "Nothing else matters."

"How can you say that?" He glanced around. "You live in a palace."

"The two weeks I spent with you were the happiest in my life." She raised her hand to his face and he immediately turned into the palm and kissed it. "I think you were happy, too. I think you've missed me."

"Like crazy."

"Then ask me to come back."

Jake closed his eyes as raw emotion clogged his throat. She was offering him everything. All he had to do was reach out and take it. "Do you think you could be happy with a guy like me?"

"That all depends. What do you have in mind?"

She wanted him to say the words.

"Forever. I have forever in mind, Ana. I love you. I love you so much," he murmured and drew her against him. Brushing his fingers through her hair, he cupped her face. "I wanted you from the moment I first saw you. Even bruised and soaked to the skin, you were so beautiful. And you were right, Ana. I haven't been able to get you out of my mind. I can't live without you.''

"Oh, Jake, I love you, too."

He wanted it all with her. "I've never had a home, Ana. A family. My own father never claimed me."

She tightened her hold on him. "You have a family now. Me."

Unable to express his gratitude in words, he lowered his head to hers and placed a tender kiss on her lips, then pulled back and was humbled by the love he saw in her eyes.

"Ana, I swear, I'll try to be the man you need."

"You already are that man. I love you, Jake. We can make a life here, or I'll go live with you at the cabin."

Overwhelmed by her faith, he bent down and kissed her. This time he wasted no time and teased her tempting mouth as his tongue delved inside for a taste. She moaned as her hands went into his hair and pulled him closer. When he broke away, they were both breathless.

"Since I have a job offer here, I think it would be wise to stay in Penwyck. That is if you'll do me the honor of marrying me." His voice was rough with desire and emotion.

Ana's smile lit up her entire face. "I was wondering if you were ever going to get around to asking. Oh, yes, Jake. I'll marry you."

He kissed her again, and again. Finally he tore his mouth away and trailed kisses down her neck. "I expect you want the big church wedding."

"No, not with my father's illness. Besides, I don't

want to wait too long.'' She smiled. ''I was hoping we could be married a little sooner. Maybe in a few weeks with just family and some friends and maybe the children from the Marlestone House. I'd like to continue my work at the orphanage.''

Smiling, he held her tight against him and placed a quick kiss on her mouth. ''Anything my princess desires.''

Epilogue

A month later, Jake drove the old truck up the road and over the rise to the cabin. He parked next to the shed and jumped out, raced around to the other side and opened the passenger door for his new bride.

When Ana had said she wanted to honeymoon at the cabin, he thought it was a crazy idea. He wanted to take her somewhere spectacular in the world, but in the end he realized she'd been right. This was the place where they met and fell in love. It was only fitting they start their new life here…together.

Dressed in a pair of slate-gray wool slacks and a burgundy sweater, Ana started to climb out of the truck when Jake scooped her up into his arms. She laughed at his romantic gesture and placed her arms around his neck.

"Oh, this is nice. But don't hurt yourself, husband, I have plans for you tonight."

He kissed her. "I wonder if they're the same as mine." He enjoyed her provocative smile as he carried her across the yard to the porch and they were greeted by Max.

"Hello, boy," Ana called. The dog wagged his tail.

"Sorry, fella," Jake began, "You'll have to wait for some attention. She's mine today."

He had waited, for over a month. During that time he'd spent days here supervising the repairs and addition made to the cabin. Things he'd meant to do when he bought the place, but hadn't gotten around to it. The prospect of a new wife pushed his plans into motion. He hadn't had much time, but with Pierce's help and laborers from Penwyck, they repaired the roof and enlarged the porch to hold a swing that held two. "I thought we could sit here and watch the sunrises and sunsets."

Ana smiled. "This is lovely. What other surprises do you have for me?"

"See for yourself." He pushed open the door and carried his bride over the threshold. Ana gasped, seeing a fire in the hearth, and several lamps had been lit, bathing the room in a soft seductive light. A snowy white cloth draped the table, which was set for two. Jake could smell the aroma of their wedding supper warming in the oven.

"Looks like elves have invaded the place," she said.

"They were pricey elves." He'd planned this for weeks. With a little help from Ana's sisters, Megan and Meredith, he'd surprised himself at how creative he could be.

Both he and Ana had had so much to do this past month. Beside wedding preparations, Ana had taken on more responsibility at Marlestone House, making the children her top priority.

He'd spent every spare moment working with the contractor on the cabin. The rest of the time, he'd stayed busy with orientating himself into his new position with the Royal Elite Team and finding out exactly what fit into his job description. He was proud to say they'd found several leads on the men who'd invaded their mountain to get the diamonds. He also had met the king's brother, the infamous Broderick. Jake hadn't been impressed with the man who was making it his life's ambition to overthrow King Morgan.

All that was forgotten this week while he and Ana began their lives together. Jake set his bride down and found he was holding his breath as she moved around the cabin. She examined the new furniture, the propane stove, then walked to the bedroom door and opened it. He heard another gasp and she swung around.

"Oh, Jake. What have you done?"

He went to her. "You don't like it?" He glanced over her shoulder into the newly remodeled bedroom. The carpenters had rebuilt the room making it almost twice its original size—big enough to fit a king-size bed, a large dresser and an overstuffed chair. Along one of the walls were bay windows above a padded seat overlooking the mountain range.

"It's beautiful. But, Jake, you didn't have to do this. I loved the cabin just as it was before."

He drew her against him. "I know, but if we're going to spend any time here, I wanted us to be comfortable." He pointed her to the opposite wall and a door. "That's why I added this."

"A closet?" Ana crossed the room, admiring the thick sand-colored carpet, wondering if Jake had picked it out. At the doorway, she gripped the knob and opened it, finding a bathroom, with a gleaming white tub, sink and a toilet. "How did you manage to do all this?"

"I had a lot of help. I thought indoor plumbing was a necessity. I hated those long walks to the outhouse. There's also a generator, so we'll have electricity and heat for those cold nights."

She walked to him. "I was hoping you'd keep me warm."

Jake grinned. "I like the way you think, chère."

Ana slid her hands up his chest and around his neck. "I like it when you call me that." She kissed him.

"I thought you hated it."

Ana couldn't recall a time when she ever hated anything about this man, unless it was his stubbornness. "I had to act indifferent at first so you wouldn't see how much I was beginning to care for you. It was you who couldn't stand having me around."

"Oh, yeah, I couldn't stand you, all right, but I couldn't resist you, either."

"I think we both were trying so hard to fight our feelings. Now, we don't have to—fight that is."

"No, we don't." He bent his head and captured her mouth. When she moved against him, he deepened the kiss, running his hand over her back and down to her bottom. When he pulled away, she could see the desire in his eyes.

"Maybe we should eat our supper now while we have the chance," he suggested as he started to lead her out of the room.

She resisted. "I'm not hungry for food…just you."

Jake wanted tonight to be special…for her. He

knew this was Ana's first time. And to be honest, he was terrified that somehow he would rush her. "Wouldn't want to waste good food."

"We can have our meal later." She stood on her tiptoes and kissed him, breaking down his resistance. He had trouble thinking about anything other than making love to her. "Unless you don't want me."

"Oh, I want you. You're all I've been thinking about since the moment I first saw you." He pulled her against him, letting her know how much. "But we better slow down. I mean it isn't even dark...."

"Goodness, Jake." She bit her lower lip to hide a smile. "I thought bridegrooms were supposed to be the anxious ones."

He kissed her, hard. "Never doubt, chère, I want you morning, noon and night. I'm crazy for you. I just want this to be perfect for you."

"Your making love to me will be perfect. Now, haven't we waited long enough?"

In answer, Jake swung her up in his arms and carried her to the bed. "Way too long, Princess. This southern boy is more than willing, but I like to take things slow and easy, prolong the pleasure."

"Oh, I like a man of action," she said in a breathy voice.

He managed to remove the blue comforter and laid her down on the sheets. He pulled off her shoes and tossed them to the floor, then went for her sweater and her slacks. He stripped away his own shirt and slacks, then climbed in next to her. He brushed her hair back and kissed her until she was whimpering. "How am I doing so far?

"You're not doing bad."

He grew serious. "Tell me what you want, chère."

Her fingers ran through his hair. "Just you, and your love…and your baby."

Emotions nearly choked him as Jake tried to find his voice.

Then Ana said, "I was hoping we could get started on expanding our family. Is that all right with you?"

"You want a baby? Now?"

She locked those sparkling blue eyes with his. "I want *your* baby, Jake, but only if that's what you want, too."

"I want that very much. I love you." He held her in a tight embrace.

Ana couldn't know the gift she was offering him, but he planned on showing her for the rest of their lives. Suddenly he was a true believer in happily ever after.

*   *   *   *   *

Keep a watch out for next month's

CROWN & GLORY

when

SEARCHING FOR HER PRINCE

*by Karen Rose Smith (SR1612)
comes to Silhouette Romance!*

Silhouette
SPECIAL EDITION™

&

SILHOUETTE *Romance*®

present a new series about the proud,
passion-driven dynasty

THE
COLTONS

**You loved the California Coltons, now discover
the Coltons of Black Arrow, Oklahoma.
Comanche blood courses through their veins,
but a brand-new birthright awaits them....**

WHITE DOVE'S PROMISE by Stella Bagwell (7/02, SE#1478)

THE COYOTE'S CRY by Jackie Merritt (8/02, SE#1484)

WILLOW IN BLOOM by Victoria Pade (9/02, SE#1490)

THE RAVEN'S ASSIGNMENT by Kasey Michaels (9/02, SR#1613)

A COLTON FAMILY CHRISTMAS by Judy Christenberry,
Linda Turner and Carolyn Zane (10/02, Silhouette Single Title)

SKY FULL OF PROMISE by Teresa Southwick (11/02, SR#1624)

THE WOLF'S SURRENDER by Sandra Steffen (12/02, SR#1630)

*Look for these titles
wherever Silhouette books are sold!*

Silhouette®
Where love comes alive™

**Where royalty and romance
go hand in hand...**

The series continues in Silhouette Romance
with these unforgettable novels:

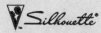

SPECIAL EDITION™

**Was it something in the water...
or something in the air?**

**Because bachelors in Bridgewater, Texas,
are becoming a vanishing breed—fast!**

**Don't miss these three exciting stories of Texas
cowboys by favorite author Jodi O'Donnell:**

Deke Larrabie returns to discover
someone *else* he left behind....
THE COME-BACK COWBOY
**(Special Edition #1494)
September 2002**

Connor Brody meets his match and gives her
THE RANCHER'S PROMISE
**(Silhouette Romance #1619)
October 2002**

Griff Corbin learns about true
friendship and love when he falls for
HIS BEST FRIEND'S BRIDE
**(Silhouette Romance #1625)
November 2002**

Available at your favorite retail outlet.

Where love comes alive™

Visit Silhouette at www.eHarlequin.com   SSEBRB

If you enjoyed what you just read,
then we've got an offer you can't resist!

Take 2 bestselling
love stories FREE!

Plus get a FREE surprise gift!

Clip this page and mail it to Silhouette Reader Service™

IN U.S.A.
3010 Walden Ave.
P.O. Box 1867
Buffalo, N.Y. 14240-1867

IN CANADA
P.O. Box 609
Fort Erie, Ontario
L2A 5X3

YES! Please send me 2 free Silhouette Romance® novels and my free surprise gift. After receiving them, if I don't wish to receive anymore, I can return the shipping statement marked cancel. If I don't cancel, I will receive 6 brand-new novels every month, before they're available in stores! In the U.S.A., bill me at the bargain price of $3.34 plus 25¢ shipping and handling per book and applicable sales tax, if any*. In Canada, bill me at the bargain price of $3.80 plus 25¢ shipping and handling per book and applicable taxes**. That's the complete price and a savings of at least 10% off the cover prices—what a great deal! I understand that accepting the 2 free books and gift places me under no obligation ever to buy any books. I can always return a shipment and cancel at any time. Even if I never buy another book from Silhouette, the 2 free books and gift are mine to keep forever.

215 SDN DNUM
315 SDN DNUN

Name	(PLEASE PRINT)	
Address	Apt.#	
City	State/Prov.	Zip/Postal Code

* Terms and prices subject to change without notice. Sales tax applicable in N.Y.
** Canadian residents will be charged applicable provincial taxes and GST.
   All orders subject to approval. Offer limited to one per household and not valid to
   current Silhouette Romance® subscribers.
   ® are registered trademarks of Harlequin Books S.A., used under license.

SROM02   ©1998 Harlequin Enterprises Limited

COMING NEXT MONTH